AN EVENT-BASED SCIENCE MODULE

HURRICANE!

STUDENT EDITION

Russell G. Wright

Innovative Learning Publications

Addison-Wesley Publishing Company

Menlo Park, California • Reading, Massachusetts • New York
Don Mills, Ontario • Wokingham, England • Amsterdam • Bonn
Paris • Milan • Madrid • Sydney • Singapore • Tokyo
Seoul • Taipei • Mexico City • San Juan

The developers of Event-Based Science have been encouraged and supported at every step in the creative process by the Superintendent and Board of Education of Montgomery County Public Schools, Rockville, Maryland (MCPS). The superintendent and board are committed to the systemic improvement of science instruction, grades preK–12. EBS is one of many projects undertaken to ensure the scientific literacy of *all* students.

The developers of *Hurricane!* pay special tribute to the editors, publisher, and reporters of *USA Today*. Without their cooperation and support the creation of this module would not have been possible.

The "Hurricane Tracking Chart" on page 22 is provided by the National Oceanic and Atmospheric Administration (NOAA).

"The Naming of Hurricanes" on page 44 is excerpted from "The Naming of Hurricanes," U.S. Dept. of Commerce, NOAA National Weather Service.

Cover Photograph: Bill Wisser, Gamma Liaison
Pages 3, 4, 43 *USA Today*; 5, 28 Bill Mills; 13, 16 NOAA; 33, 34 AP/Wide World Photos; all "Student Voices" photographs John Wickham.
Project Editor: Katarina Stenstedt
Production/Manufacturing: Leanne Collins
Design Manager: Jeff Kelly
Text and Cover Design: Frank Loose Design, Portland, Oregon

This book is published by Innovative Learning Publications™, an imprint of the Alternative Publishing Group of Addison-Wesley Publishing Company.

This material is based upon work supported by the National Science Foundation under grant number MDR-9154094. Any opinions, findings, conclusions, or recommendations expressed in this publication are those of the Event-Based Science Project and do not necessarily reflect the views of the National Science Foundation.

Contents

Preface

The Event-Based Science Model

Hurricane! is a student booklet about meteorology that follows the Event-Based Science (EBS) instructional model. You will begin by watching "live" television news coverage of Hurricane Andrew and reading *USA Today* reports about it. Your discussions about the hurricane will show you and your teacher that you already know a lot about the meteorological concepts of the event. Next, a real-world task puts you and your classmates in the roles of people who must use scientific knowledge and processes to solve a problem related to hurricanes. You will probably need more information before you start the task. If you do, this book provides hands-on activities and a variety of reading materials to give you some of the background you will need. About halfway through the unit, you will be ready to begin the task. Your teacher will assign you a role to play and turn you and your team loose to complete the task. You will spend the rest of the time in this unit working on that task.

Scientific Literacy

Today, a literate citizen is expected to know more than how to read, write, and do simple arithmetic. Today, literacy includes knowing how to analyze problems, ask critical questions, and explain events. A literate citizen must also be able to apply scientific knowledge and processes in new situations. Event-Based Science allows you to practice these skills by placing the study of science in a meaningful context.

Knowledge cannot be transferred to your mind from the mind of your teacher, or from the pages of a textbook. Nor can knowledge occur in isolation from the other things you know about and have experienced in the real world. The Event-Based Science model is based on the idea that the best way to know something is to be actively engaged in it.

Therefore, the Event-Based Science model simulates real-life events and experiences to make your learning more authentic and memorable. First, the event is brought to life through television news coverage. Viewing the news allows you to be there "as it happened," and that is as close as you can get to actually experiencing the event. Second, by simulating the kinds of teamwork and problem solving that occur every day in our workplaces and communities, you will experience the role that scientific knowledge and teamwork play in the lives of ordinary people. Thus the book is built around real-life events and experiences that affected people's lives and environments dramatically.

In an Event-Based Science classroom, you become the workers. Your product is a solution to a real problem, and your teacher is your coach, guide, and advisor. You will be assessed on how you use scientific processes and concepts to solve problems and on the quality of your work.

One of the primary goals of the EBS Project is to place the learning of science in a real-world context and to make scientific learning fun. You should not allow yourself to become frustrated. If you cannot find a specific piece of information, it's okay to be creative. For example, if you are working as the reporter for your team and you cannot find the actual names of shopping centers, streets, factories, and housing developments, use your imagination, but keep it realistic. Base your response on the real places you know about. Just remember to identify your creation as fictional.

Student Resources

This module is unlike a regular textbook. An Event-Based Science module tells a story about a real event. It has real newspaper articles about the event and inserts that explain the scientific concepts involved in the event. It also contains laboratory investigations for you to conduct in your science class and activities you may do in English, math, social studies, or technology-education classes. In addition, an Event-Based Science module gives you and your classmates a real-world task to do. The task is always done by teams of students, with each team member performing a real-life role while completing an important part of the task. The task cannot be completed without you and everyone else on your team doing their parts. The team approach allows you to share your knowledge and strengths. It also helps you learn to work with a team in a real-world situation. Today, most professionals work in teams.

Interviews with people who actually serve in the roles you are playing are scattered throughout the Event-Based Science module. Middle school students who actually experienced the event tell their stories throughout the module too.

Since this module is unlike a regular textbook, you have much more flexibility in using it.

- You may read **The Story** for enjoyment or to find clues that will help you tackle your part of the task.

- You may read selections from the **Discovery File** when you need help understanding something in the story or when you need help with the task.

- You may read all the **On the Job** features because you are curious about what professionals do, or you may read only the interview with the professional who works in the role you've chosen because it may give you ideas that will help you complete the task.

- You may read the **In the News** features because they catch your eye, or as part of your search for information.

- You will probably read all the **Student Voices** features because they are interesting stories told by middle-school students like yourself.

Hurricane! is also unlike regular textbooks in that the collection of resources found in it is not meant to be complete. You must find additional information from other sources too. Textbooks, encyclopedias, maps, pamphlets, magazine and newspaper articles, videos, films, filmstrips, computer databases, and people in your community are all potential sources of useful information. It is vital to your preparation as a scientifically literate citizen of the twenty-first century that you get used to finding information on your own.

The shape of a new form of science education is beginning to emerge, and the Event-Based Science Project is leading the way. We hope you enjoy your experience with this module as much as we enjoyed developing it.

—Russell G. Wright, Ed.D.,
Project Director and Principal Author

A Hurricane's Humble Beginnings

It is hard to believe that a hurricane has humble beginnings. In mid-August of 1992, just off the west coast of Africa, ocean waters were being warmed by the sun overhead. High above the wide expanse of warm sea water, the sky became dotted with billowy clouds as a low-pressure system entered the area, gracefully riding into the region of the trade winds.

The low-pressure weather system, the central core of which was warmer than the surrounding atmosphere, churned up strong winds as it traveled across the ocean's surface. Usually these subtle ripples in the atmosphere ride out over the tropical Atlantic Ocean and die a natural death. Very few of these weather systems have the power to become a tropical storm, and even fewer have the muscle and speed to turn into a full-fledged hurricane like Andrew.

But on August 14, 1992, this then nameless convergence of air, ocean, humidity, and temperature gave birth to one of the most devastating weather events ever to strike the United States. Three days later, with winds speeding along at 39 miles per hour, the small but ferocious storm was given the preliminary name Tropical Storm Andrew. The Atlantic breeding ground for bad weather had produced the first Atlantic tropical storm of the 1992 hurricane season.

Between August 17 and August 20, Tropical Storm Andrew turned from west to west-north-west, which placed it on a destructive path toward the Lesser Antilles, also known as the West Indian Islands. An upper-level low-pressure system also in the atmosphere, however, caused Andrew to reduce its speed, and steered the storm toward a northwesterly course. That change in direction spared the Lesser Antilles from holding an encounter of their own with Andrew.

Just two days later, on August 22, Andrew turned due west. As an area of low atmospheric pressure, Andrew's swirl of winds and clouds drew energy from the warm ocean surface. Spinning in a counter-clockwise direction, the blend of clouds and wind circled a cloudless core—the very eye of the storm system. As its winds accelerated,

➤ continued on page 2

➤ continued from page 1

Andrew reached hurricane strength and became the first Atlantic hurricane to form from a tropical wave of energy in nearly two years. ■

Discussion Questions:

1. What are hurricanes and what causes them?

2. What do you think it is about our part of the country that accounts for the fact that we (pick one) (A) frequently, (B) occasionally, (C) seldom, (D) never experience hurricanes?

3. There are other forms of violent weather that affect our region. Make a list of the violent weather events that our region experiences, ranking them in order from those that occur most frequently to those that are least frequent.

4. What is the most important way that weather affects your life?

The winds were so strong that my shutters were coming loose. I yelled to my father, "Watch out, I hear something coming." He moved away from the window just as a big pine tree flew in. The tree curved up and flew out through the roof like a rocket. When the tree flew through the roof, the whole roof unraveled like a roll of tape.

NOEL MARTINEZ
PERRINE, FL

IN THE NEWS

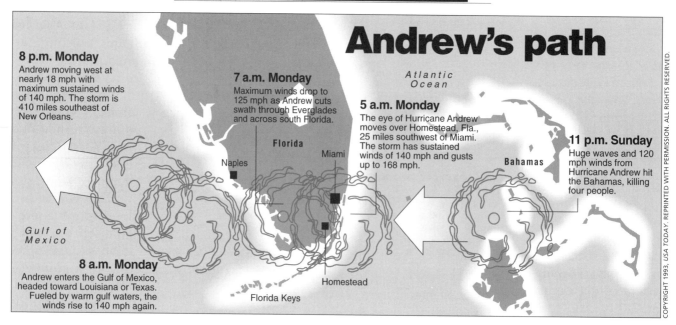

Andrew's path

8 p.m. Monday
Andrew moving west at nearly 18 mph with maximum sustained winds of 140 mph. The storm is 410 miles southeast of New Orleans.

7 a.m. Monday
Maximum winds drop to 125 mph as Andrew cuts swath through Everglades and across south Florida.

Atlantic Ocean

5 a.m. Monday
The eye of Hurricane Andrew moves over Homestead, Fla., 25 miles southwest of Miami. The storm has sustained winds of 140 mph and gusts up to 168 mph.

11 p.m. Sunday
Huge waves and 120 mph winds from Hurricane Andrew hit the Bahamas, killing four people.

Florida

Naples

Miami

Bahamas

Gulf of Mexico

8 a.m. Monday
Andrew enters the Gulf of Mexico, headed toward Louisiana or Texas. Fueled by warm gulf waters, the winds rise to 140 mph again.

Homestead

Florida Keys

Andrew hits Florida

Biggest storm in decades homes in on the coast

By H. Darr Beiser, USA TODAY

USA TODAY, 24 AUGUST 1992

EVACUATED: Miami area residents jam into North Miami Beach High School Sunday.

By Robert Davis
and Jack Williams
USA TODAY

CORAL GABLES, Fla. — Hurricane Andrew chased as many as a million people from their homes then descended on south Florida today.

Andrew's edge hit the coast at 1:15 a.m. ET today, threatening to wreak havoc with winds between 135 and 150 mph, heavy rain and 18-foot waves.

Evacuations were ordered Sunday after Andrew hit the

Bahamas, killing at least four.

The last bus left Miami Beach at midnight. Kim Miller of Dade County emergency center warned those left to "just snuggle up for the night."

Andrew's eye was expected to hit Miami, but a 250-mile area from Key West to Fort Lauderdale was evacuated.

Those staying face misdemeanor charges, but most residents took Andrew seriously.

"Those coconuts are like cannon balls," says Jim McDermott, 65, who fled with

his grandchildren. "They can blast through concrete."

Officials warn Andrew could become only the third Category 5 hurricane — the strongest possible — on record and the only one since 1969.

If Andrew stays its course, it will rip across Florida and roar into the Gulf of Mexico between Naples and Fort Myers.

In Florida Sunday:
▶ Gov. Lawton Chiles declared an emergency and asked President Bush to declare a federal disaster area.

▶ Airports closed; hundreds of flights were canceled.
▶ Officials drained hundreds of miles of canals, hoping to prevent flooding.
▶ The Federal Emergency Management Agency and 27 other groups geared up.
▶ The National Guard had 1,500 troops standing by.
▶ A third of the experts from the National Hurricane Center here went to a backup center near Washington, D.C.
▶ AT&T limited incoming calls, giving calls out priority.

Andrew zeros in again

South Fla. looks like 'bomb' hit

USA TODAY, 25 AUGUST 1992

By Sharon Donovan
and Steve Marshall
USA TODAY

NEW ORLEANS — Hurricane Andrew, bearing down on the Gulf Coast today, leaves behind a stunned and staggering south Florida.

The storm battered the peninsula with 140 mph winds and gusts up to 168 mph early Monday, flattening everything in its path. Death toll: at least 10.

"I don't know how you describe the devastation," said Gov. Lawton Chiles. "It looks like an air bomb went off."

Emergency officials estimated 50,000 were left homeless.

Homestead, Fla., south of Miami and not included in the evacuation plan, was nearly demolished. Military personnel had no comment on reports that Homestead Air Force Base was destroyed.

Chiles deployed nearly 2,000 National Guard personnel to help with relief and stop looting. Local authorities issued a 7 p.m.-to-7 a.m. curfew.

The storm, the most powerful to strike Florida since 1935, cut power to 1.3 million people.

As Floridians begin to regroup, 1 million New Orleans-

area residents started evacuating their low-lying homes.

They fear a direct hit when Andrew comes ashore again, possibly as early as tonight.

"We are all on alert," said Louisiana Gov. Edwin Edwards after mobilizing the National Guard Monday.

"The evacuation of the city of New Orleans has always been our worst nightmare from an emergency planning standpoint," said state police Capt. Ronnie Jones.

"Escape routes are virtually non-existent," said Robert Watts of Tulane University.

Cloud Formation

From the ground, clouds can look like huge piles of cotton or billowing mounds of whipped cream. But if you've ever flown through a cloud in an airplane or hiked at very high altitudes, you know that clouds are more like great areas of clammy, gray fog. This should not surprise us, because clouds—like fog—are made up of water droplets suspended in air.

Molecules of water vapor move about in the air, rising as the air grows warm. But as air rises, it eventually grows cooler. The air temperature drops 3 degrees C (Celsius) for every 300 meters, or 5.4 degrees F (Fahrenheit) for every 1000 feet

of rise. As the rising air cools, condensation occurs and the tiny water droplets born of that condensation form a cloud.

These tiny droplets condense onto solid particles drifting around in the atmosphere, particles of sea salt, dust, or pollen, for example, picked up by the wind as it blows over the earth. And of course, as water vapor continues to reach its condensation level, additional water droplets attach themselves to the surrounding particles, increasing the density and area of the cloud.

Why do some clouds look white, and others gray or even black? Some clouds are white because their water droplets or

ice crystals are just the right size to scatter light of all wavelengths. First, understand that sunlight contains all the colors of the rainbow. Light travels as waves, each color possessing its own unique wavelength. When light of all wavelengths is scattered, the colors combine to produce white light.

Clouds can appear dark for several different reasons. They can be very dense with water droplets, or very thick, so that they block the rays of sunlight. The top part of a cloud could also cast a shadow on its own base, or it could be in the shadow of a higher cloud. So don't assume that dark clouds are always rain clouds.

Hurricane Warnings

BY **DAVE BARRY**

As you are probably aware, especially if you are one of those people whose major appliances are still up in trees, South Florida recently experienced a bad hurricane. So today, as a South Florida homeowner, I want to review some of the lessons I learned from this experience—lessons that I believe can be useful not only in hurricanes, but in other natural disasters such as floods, earthquakes, and children's birthday parties.

The most important precaution, for a homeowner facing a natural disaster, is:

1. SELL YOUR HOUSE BEFORE THE NATURAL DISASTER OCCURS.

Trust me, this simple step will save you a LOT of trouble. My wife, Beth, and I are still kicking ourselves for not doing it. When we heard that Hurricane Andrew was headed directly at us, we rushed around doing things like putting patio furniture inside, securing doors, etc. What a pair of morons. We should have used that time to sell the house to somebody, and let HIM worry about the patio furniture.

Granted, at that point there probably was not a large pool of qualified buyers available, so we might not have gotten absolute top dollar:

Us: So, do we have a deal here?

Prospective Buyer: Let me get this straight. I get your house, and you get ... my BIKE?

Us: (driving a hard bargain): AND your skateboard.

Prospective Buyer: I have to ask my mom.

If you're foolish enough to keep your home, you should definitely:

2. SEARCH THE HOME FOR WORKING DRUM SETS AND DESTROY THEM WITH AN AX.

We weathered the hurricane in the home of some friends who are normally sane people, but who had allowed their 11-year-old son, Trey, to purchase a used drum set THE DAY BEFORE THE HURRICANE. Here's the thing about drums: They don't need electricity. They are designed to function perfectly during a natural disaster. This meant that at 2 A.M., when the power went out and the night was black and the wind was shrieking and the eye was approaching and we were sitting in the darkness, rigid with tension, terrified about what was about to happen, fearful that the house might BANG BANG BANG BANG WHAMMMA WHAMMMA WHAMMMA OHMIGOD WHAT'S HAPPENING?!!?

Ha ha! It was only young Trey, sensing somehow that this was a superb time to practice. So we all had a good laugh, and there is a strong chance that some of our hearts will eventually resume beating.

3. DESTROY YOUR GARDEN HOSE.

Few people realize how dangerous a garden hose can be. I found out while attempting to siphon gasoline into a chain saw so I could locate our house, which was somewhere inside a mass of fallen trees approximately the size of Cambodia.

We had obtained the chain saw from these men who sprang up all over the place, mushroom-like, immediately after the storm. They were selling truckloads of powerful, potentially lethal chain saws to South Florida homeowners whose experience with dangerous tools was pretty much limited to corkscrews. I watched a TV reporter ask one of the chain-saw sellers if he had any Safety Tips for the viewing audience. The man thought for a second, then said, quote: "Chain saw don't know the difference between a LAIG and a LAWG."

Bearing that Safety Tip in mind, I unpacked my new chain saw and determined, using mechanical aptitude, that you had to put gasoline in it. I decided to siphon some out of my wife's car. My wife's car is her pride and joy, and it spent the hurricane inside the garage; a tree landed on the garage, but the car was undamaged. So I cut off a length of garden hose, and I stuck it down the car's gas pipe, and—I bet this NEVER happens to criminals—it got stuck in there. When I tried to pull it back out, it broke. Which meant there was four feet of alien garden hose somewhere deep inside my wife's car. And you just KNOW the mechanic is going to tell me that the only way to fix it is to replace the engine, perhaps several times.

This is why you need National Guard troops in disaster areas. I needed a National Guard troop to come into my garage right then and shoot me in the head. That would have spared me from having to go into the house to tell my wife that on this day—a day when our trees had been knocked down and our roof damaged and our other car bashed up by roof tiles and our entire neighborhood strewn with debris and our roads blocked and our power knocked out for what looked like several weeks—that on this day, the first thing I had done, the first step on the long road to recovery, was to screw up her car.

When I explain this to the mechanic, he'd better not laugh at me. I'm going to have the chain saw running by then.

©1992, DAVE BARRY. REPRINTED WITH PERMISSION.

We had about eight people, ten animals, a bird cage, and a dog in our closet. Trees were falling down and the house was starting to shake. We could hear everything. I started getting sick, I was so scared. When we looked outside the door, there was water coming down. It was raining inside the house! Then, all of a sudden, we felt water coming up from the floor. Everybody was screaming.

LAUREN SWERDLOFF
KENDALL, FL

DISCOVERY FILE

Air Pressure

It may be hard to believe, but the weight of the atmosphere is constantly pressing on you. Every square inch of your skin receives approximately 14.7 pounds of pressure at sea level, less at higher elevations. At 18,000 feet the pressure drops to 7.3 pounds per square inch. We don't notice this change in pressure on our skin, but we do notice it. Our eardrums are especially sensitive to rapid changes in air pressure as we drive up a mountain or climb higher in an airplane.

What causes air pressure, and what does it have to do with weather? Though you can't see it, air is real. It takes up space and has mass. Things that take up space and have mass are called *matter*, and matter is made of molecules. Air molecules, mostly nitrogen and oxygen, are moving about at incredible speeds all around us. In fact, near the earth's surface, they are traveling at more than 1000 miles per hour. The impact of all those molecules zipping around at such high speeds is what causes pressure. The more collisions, the higher the pressure. We don't feel this high-speed bombardment as wind because the molecules are moving in different directions. In fact, we don't even feel the bombardment as pressure unless it changes suddenly.

To understand how air pressure is related to weather, read the discussion of wind on page 8.

Wind

The air surrounding the earth is almost always in motion. When it moves slowly, we call that movement a breeze. When it moves so fast we can't stand up, we call it a *gale* or *hurricane*. But what makes the wind blow at all?

To understand the answer, keep in mind this basic principle: warmed air rises and expands because when air is warmed the air molecules spread out. Air molecules found above cold surfaces are much more closely packed together. So hot air is less dense and therefore lighter than the same amount of cold air at the same level.

Now, imagine the sun as it travels across the sky. As it passes over some parts of the sea and land, it warms certain spots more than others. Darker surfaces absorb more of the sun's energy than do lighter colored surfaces. As energy is absorbed, the temperature rises. The air above these hot spots rises too, and cool air rushes in to fill the void. This kind of movement is called *convection*. As convection continues, an area of low pressure forms under the rising warm air, and a corresponding high pressure area forms under the sinking cooler air.

This difference of density and pressure over continents and oceans, and between hot and cold areas, makes the air move and thus sets the winds blowing.

Imagine, for example, the temperature differences between the equator and the poles. As you might expect, the warm air at the equator tends to rise and be replaced by cold air moving in underneath it from the poles. These pressure differences create a general movement of air worldwide. Air movement thus provides a moderating effect on the otherwise extreme temperatures at the equator and the poles.

How is it, then, that global winds tend to circle around the globe rather than flowing in straight lines from north to south? The answer is that these winds are turned by the Coriolis effect. Nineteenth century French scientist G. G. Coriolis observed that because of the earth's rotation, winds in the Northern Hemisphere are deflected to the right, while those in the Southern Hemisphere are thrown off to the left.

It is this force that explains why the air in certain air masses, including high-pressure air masses, spins in the Northern Hemisphere in a clockwise direction, and revolves in the Southern Hemisphere in a counterclockwise direction. Coriolis noted that the faster the wind is moving, the greater the deflection. A complicated interaction between the Coriolis force and the force of the pressure itself causes low-pressure air masses to spin in a direction opposite to that of high-pressure air masses, that is, counterclockwise in the Northern Hemisphere and clockwise in the Southern Hemisphere.

Much of the Earth's weather depends on a system of winds that blow in more or less expected directions. You have probably heard of the jet stream, a narrow band of high-altitude wind that blows from west to east at about 60 mph in the summer, and at about 150 mph in the winter—a time when there is the greatest temperature contrast between the polar regions and more temperate areas. The jet stream does not circle the poles smoothly but loops down into more temperate zones, sometimes bringing air from the North Pole almost as far south as the tropics.

In hotter tropical regions there is often only a slight breeze, and winds change direction often. This area is called the *doldrums*. This was a dangerous area when ships of old sailed the seas, for they could be becalmed for weeks. The doldrums are found at about 20 to 30 degrees latitude north and south of the equator. Sailors called these belts of calm high-pressure air circling the globe the Horse Latitudes, for the horses that sometimes died of thirst when the sailing ships that carried them languished for lack of wind.

Other winds particularly important to these same sailors of old were the trade winds which generally blow from the northeast to the southwest in the Northern Hemisphere. Sailing-ship captains leaving Europe sailed far enough south to catch

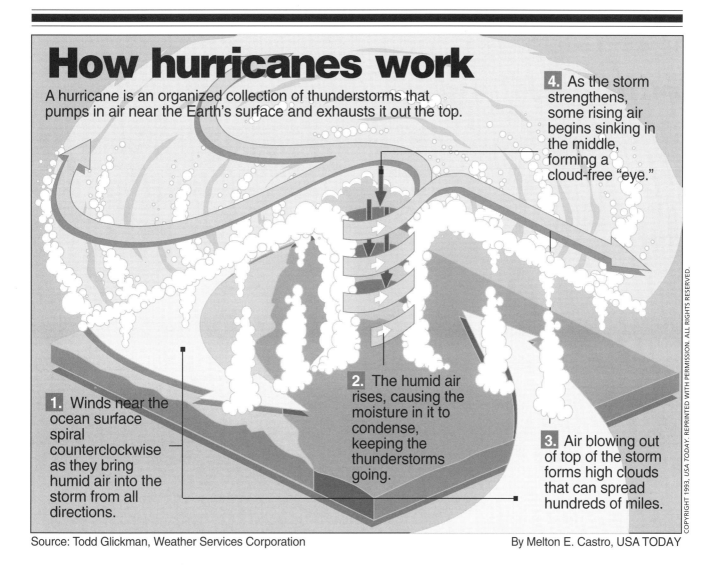

How hurricanes work

A hurricane is an organized collection of thunderstorms that pumps in air near the Earth's surface and exhausts it out the top.

4. As the storm strengthens, some rising air begins sinking in the middle, forming a cloud-free "eye."

1. Winds near the ocean surface spiral counterclockwise as they bring humid air into the storm from all directions.

2. The humid air rises, causing the moisture in it to condense, keeping the thunderstorms going.

3. Air blowing out of top of the storm forms high clouds that can spread hundreds of miles.

Source: Todd Glickman, Weather Services Corporation

By Melton E. Castro, USA TODAY

the steady trade winds that would then carry them westward into the Caribbean. When they were ready to return to Europe, they sailed northward along the North American coast until they found the Westerlies, trade winds which curve eastward as they headed north.

The monsoon is also part of the planetary wind system. Monsoons occur when air pressure over a large area reverses itself as seasons change. For example, central India is extremely hot from March to June. The hot air rises, and moist air from the nearby Indian Ocean moves in to take its place.

This creates the wet summer monsoon. The reverse happens in winter, when the air above the sea is warmer than air above the land. The cool dry air from the Indian interior moves in to replace the warm air rising above the Indian ocean.

In addition to the planetary wind system, local winds affect smaller areas. One such regional wind is that of land breezes and sea breezes. During the day the land warms up more than the sea. The warm air rises, making way for a sea breeze, as the cool air over the sea flows in to replace the warm air. At night, the pattern is reversed.

The land cools more quickly than the water, so the warmer air over the sea rises, and cool air from land flows out to replace it. This flow of air from land to sea is called a *land breeze.*

Another local wind system is a mountain wind. Mountain slopes, especially those made of bare rock, are heated by the sun during the day. The warm air rises, and more air flows upward from valleys to fill its place. This creates an updraft along the sides of mountains during the afternoon. The reverse occurs at night, as the mountain slope cools, and heavier cold air flows back down into the valleys.

Editor-in-Chief

JOHN WOLFF
FLAVOR MAGAZINE
WASHINGTON, DC

I am 23 years old. I am Publisher and Editor-in-Chief of *Flavor* magazine. This is a tremendous responsibility. As far as I'm concerned, Editor-in-Chief is the most important job you can have in this project. The buck stops with the Editor-in-Chief. If a newspaper is bad, it's the Editor-in-Chief's fault. He or she has total control of what goes into the paper. But if the newspaper is good, he or she will probably receive little praise.

There were always magazines in my house when I was growing up. I started reading them and became a magazine junky. In 1988, I came to Washington, D.C., to study at American University. I noticed I couldn't get the kinds of magazines in Washington that I could get in New York. So, I decided that I'd better start my own.

The newspaper business is very scary, especially the night before printing. But you have the instant gratification of seeing what you did—what you did right, and what you did wrong—the next morning. It's a very quick turnaround. You will make a lot of mistakes, but eventually you get it right. Once you learn to control the pressure, you will be able to use it in a positive way. Pressure is a great motivator. It is said that "every great problem is also a great opportunity." If you can handle the pressures, you'll be a success. For me, a physical

challenge relieves stress. Rock climbing, marathon running, and bicycle racing are the three activities I use.

What I like best about my job is the recognition I get in the community. I like serving the community and influencing people. It makes me feel like I'm changing their views.

I don't know how to operate a printing press, but I have a lot of respect for the pressmen who do the "grunt" work, working long shifts and getting ink all over their hands. They do the hard work and make the magazine look good.

If you like the newspaper business, you should focus on reading and writing classes. A journalism class is a nice bonus if your high school has it. It's important to know mathematics, because very often you're going to be working with numbers (for example, finances, advertising, laying out a page, and billing). Science and social studies are important so that you can know what's going on in the world. Social sciences, demographic trends, and psychology can help a lot in publishing and editing.

It's also important to know how the printing process works, and the chemistry involved with getting ink on a page.

Technological advances are changing the way people think of the printing industry. Because of people's environmental concerns about saving trees, there's a lot of recycled paper used. Instead of using petroleum ink, we are using soybean ink. I have read that we will soon stop using water in the printing process.

My advice to the Editor-in-Chief is, never forget two things. First, you are the leader and you have to motivate your team. Focus on the strengths of others and compensate for their weaknesses. Secondly, always remember that everything you do is for the benefit of the reader. If there is no public to serve, there will be no newspaper.

A Hurricane Newspaper

The written word is powerful. Words inspire joy, like a letter from a close friend, or the words of your favorite song. Words generate fear, and cause sorrow. And sometimes words transmit information to people in desperate need.

When a natural disaster threatens, words have the power to save millions of lives. You and your team of expert writers, managers, and scientists have the opportunity— and the responsibility— to make a difference in the lives of the residents of your community. For some people facing devastation, you may hold the lifeline that will determine if they will live or die.

You have now seen the devastation left in the wake of Hurricane Andrew in the Bahamas, Florida, and Louisiana. The storm destroyed 25,524 homes, damaged 101,241 others, left 250,000 people homeless, and killed 54 people.

If your newspaper team had been in the path of Andrew, could you have prevented some of the deaths and saved homes?

Publishing a Newspaper After a Hurricane

You and your colleagues will be working to publish a three-page newspaper explaining the impact of a hurricane that is bearing down on "your" community.

Page one: HEADLINE HURRICANE NEWS includes general information about hurricanes and daily reports of hurricane movements.

Page two: LOCAL WEATHER and EMERGENCY PREPAREDNESS provides analysis of national and local weather conditions, situation updates, and emergency management information.

Page three: LIFE includes human interest stories and environmental damage reports.

The final products—each team's newspaper—will be displayed in the classroom and will be considered in your unit evaluation.

Coordinating your team's efforts is your Editor-in-Chief, who will also be in charge of designing a logo and banner for the newspaper, a cartoon or a humorous article, and an advertisement.

Your team's Hurricane Specialist will track a hurricane, analyzing and predicting its path and intensity as it bears down on your city.

The Meteorologist will help the Hurricane Specialist and will write articles to help readers understand and use weather maps.

The Natural Hazards Planner will provide articles on preparing for a hurricane and evacuation, if necessary, as well as public information updates during the aftermath of the hurricane that include vital information about availability of water, food, medical aid, and other services.

The Reporter will be capturing first-hand accounts of hurricane experiences through interviews with hurricane survivors. He or she will also write articles about damage to your city's roads and utilities, as well as the costs and time required to restore services to normal.

Your Environmental Scientist will write articles about the impact of storm surge on the coastal areas and investigating the problem of protecting drinking water supplies.

STUDENT VOICES

Before the hurricane hit, I wanted to be in it because I wanted to see what it was like; but afterwards I didn't want to be there.

TIFFANY WOLFER
CUTLER RIDGE, FL

Each of your class's five teams will "adopt" one of the following cities:

City, State	Zip Code
Atlantic City, New Jersey	08401
Biloxi, Mississippi	39530
Cape Hatteras, North Carolina	27948
Cedar Key, Florida	32625
Corpus Christi, Texas	78401
Galveston, Texas	77550
Mobile, Alabama	36601
New Haven, Connecticut	06501
Panama City, Florida	32401
Pensacola, Florida	32501
Port Arthur, Texas	77640

Each team will compose a letter requesting information about their city from the appropriate chamber of commerce. If you ask the chamber of commerce to send the information as soon as possible and mail your letter by the third day of the unit, you should receive the information by the time you need it.

During class discussion, identify gaps in your background knowledge and tell your teacher what you need to know before you can start the project.

Although your class has been divided into six-member teams, there are common tasks for each category of expert. These experts—for example, all the Meteorologists—will meet together to investigate their part of the overall project. This is a cooperative learning technique called *Jigsaw*.

As you play the role of the expert, you will realize that there are many important considerations when confronted with a disaster. There is a good chance that sometime in the future you will face a

STUDENT VOICES

When the hurricane first hit, we were in the bathroom. When Mom realized there was a window in the bathroom, we moved into the linen closet and stayed there with games and a flashlight. Where we were sitting, we could feel the walls shaking like rubber. We thought everything was gone.

SONDRA BUDDE
KENDALL, FL

hurricane, earthquake, tornado, or other disaster where your decisions could save lives.

Choosing Your Expert Role

Each city newspaper staff will produce its own three-page newspaper illustrating and explaining the impact of a hurricane on their "adopted" community. Each team will be composed of the following six experts:

Editor-in-Chief
Hurricane Specialist
Meteorologist
Natural Hazards Planner
Reporter
Environmental Scientist

You and your colleagues will each submit a prioritized list to your teacher with your role preferences (first, second, third choices, and so on). First choices will be given wherever possible.

Before you decide, read over the Expert Task descriptions and make sure you are willing and able to meet the responsibilities of the role. Your newspaper colleagues will be counting on you.

Once you begin the task of writing the newspaper, your teacher will provide your team with hurricane data for a real hurricane that made landfall at—or whose winds, storm surge, and/or path affected—your city.

Expert Tasks

Editor-in-Chief

1. coordinate team production of the newspaper; set deadlines to ensure timely completion of the task; keep records of what needs to be done and what has been

completed; supervise storage of parts of the newspaper, distribution and collection of materials, and clean-up
2. design a logo and banner for the newspaper
3. create an advertisement for a new product that would be valuable to people living in hurricane territory
4. write a humorous article or design a cartoon depicting some aspect of the hurricane event
5. work with the reporter to incorporate advertisement and humor(3 and 4) into the page three layout
6. read all articles and edit if necessary

Hurricane Specialist
1. make a cross-sectional diagram of a hurricane, identifying major components such as eye, clouds, wind direction and pattern, and rainfall
2. predict changes in hurricane intensity and direction, issue watches and warnings as your hurricane approaches, and prepare a chronological record of the watches and warnings you issued
3. track hurricane movements on a large map beginning five days before the hurricane strikes the city

4. write feature articles about hurricane formation and movement, including an estimate of the frequency with which hurricanes strike your city
5. work with the Editor to lay out page one of the newspaper
6. read all articles and edit if necessary

Meteorologist
1. write an article, complete with diagrams, explaining how to read a weather map
2. make a three-day series of local weather maps illustrating changes in national and local weather as your hurricane approaches
3. prepare a small map tracking hurricane movements to accompany your article
4. make a chart or table of the most economically devastating hurricanes comparing damage, deaths, and economic loss due to hurricane intensity (categories I–V)
5. work with the Editor and Natural Hazards Planner to lay out page two of the newspaper
6. read all articles and edit if necessary

Natural Hazards Planner

1. develop a hurricane home-safety emergency management plan
2. prepare emergency evacuation plan including a map identifying the locations of emergency shelters
3. design a chart or table for the newspaper that motivates people to take necessary precautions before storms, to reduce the risk of contamination during storms, and educates the public on steps they can take to purify their water
4. write newspaper articles with public information updates about aftermath, including available services, school closings, businesses open/closed, extent of damage, response to damage, availability of water, food, medical aid
5. work with the Editor and Meteorologist to lay out page two of the newspaper
6. read all articles and edit if necessary

Reporter

1. write a news report based on interviews and/or written accounts of the reactions of hurricane survivors
2. write a creative news story about the ways people have explained hurricane phenomena in the past
3. compile a fact-based, but fictitious, article about the extent of hurricane damage to the city's roads and utilities, predicting the costs and time required to restore services to normal (Use real names of streets, buildings, factories and other landmarks if you have that information from the chamber of commerce)
4. work with the Environmental Scientist to lay out page three of the newspaper
5. work with the Editor-in-Chief to incorporate advertisement and humor into page three layout
6. read all articles and edit if necessary

Environmental Scientist

1. make a map of the coastal area of the city, identify likely problem areas, and show the effects of geological features (for example, barrier islands, spits, and so on).
2. write an editorial or letter to the editor describing your plan for reducing environmental damage from future storms
3. write an article about the impact of hurricanes on freshwater supplies and ways to protect drinking water from hurricane damage
4. prepare guidelines for obtaining safe drinking water
5. work with the Reporter to lay out page three of the newspaper
6. read all articles and edit if necessary ∎

Hurricane Andrew's Windy Rain of Terror

As the eye of the hurricane took shape in the center of the giant whirlwind, Andrew intensified in power. Late in the evening of August 23, the eye of Hurricane Andrew passed over northern Eleuthera Island in the Bahamas and then hit the southern Berry Islands. Huge waves and blustery 120 mph winds whipped over the islands, leaving four dead in their wake.

As the worst hurricane to pelt the islands in over sixty years, Andrew left some seventeen hundred Bahamians homeless. Bridges, roads, and tourist hotels were wiped out. Hardest hit was the island of Eleuthera. The loss of resort hotels greatly affected the Bahamian economy as nearly 60 percent of the island nation's economy relies on tourism, with seven out of ten jobs dependent on the vacationing traveler.

But Hurricane Andrew's destructive binge in the Bahamas was only a prelude as it barreled toward the United States mainland. Emergency preparations began. Massive evacuations were ordered, not only in Florida, but also in Louisiana and in certain counties of Texas. In total, an estimated 2,733,500 people began evacuation procedures. Residents in the possible pathway of Hurricane Andrew rushed to prepare their homes for the onslaught of seriously bad weather; plywood shutters were hammered into place over windows, and boats were moved upriver or pulled out of the water. Panic set in. Worried townspeople rushed grocery stores, money machines, and gas stations as they traveled inland to safer territory. Airports ceased operations in South Florida; four nuclear reactors situated on the Florida coastline were shut down. The wait for Hurricane Andrew had begun.

Weakened by its pass over the western portion of the Great Bahama Bank, Hurricane Andrew moved westward toward southeast Florida. Hurricane-watching tools such as radar, aircraft,

➤ continued on page 16

First we were in my parents' bedroom but the patio overhang flew off and crashed through the window. So we went into the closet. We thought the closet would be strong enough, but when the roof looked like it was going to cave in, we went into the garage. My uncle from Jamaica said we should be in the car, because the car would be stronger than any other part of the house. While we were in the car, the ceiling and one of the walls of the garage caved in. Everything was dark and we couldn't see anything. At first I was really scared, but after a while I thought there is nothing I can do about this. I'm stuck in this car, and there's no sense in worrying.

XAVIER THOMAS
SOUTH MIAMI, FL

> continued from page 15

and satellites collectively verified that Hurricane Andrew was re-intensifying rapidly. As the storm was approaching Florida's coast, the warm ocean surface pumped added energy into Andrew.

Just six hours later, after crossing over the Bahamas, the eye of Hurricane Andrew moved over Homestead, Florida, a mere 25 miles southwest of Miami. At that landfall locale, ground instruments measured the hurricane's power. Although these instruments were soon destroyed by Andrew, the National Hurricane Center estimates that maximum sustained surface winds at landfall were 145 mph with gusts to at least 175 mph. One wind gauge atop a tower south of Miami recorded 177 mph gusts. It was later found that some pockets of Hurricane Andrew's winds appeared to have moved heavy concrete and steel beams. The beams, weighing tons, were transported through the air for yards, indicating winds possibly as high as 200 mph.

Analysis of data from several barometers near Homestead, Florida, measured Andrew's strength at 926 millibars—a metric measure of barometric pressure. The lower the barometric pressure, the stronger the storm. These instruments gauged Hurricane Andrew as a Category 4 storm. A Category 1 storm causes "minimal" damage, while a Category 5—the highest ranking—causes "catastrophic" damage. This classification is based on the Saffir-Simpson Damage-Potential Scale, the invention of an engineer and a meteorologist who teamed up in the early 1970s to develop a way to rate hurricanes.

Once over land, Andrew moved nearly due west and crossed the extreme southern portion of the Florida peninsula. Andrew's fury was lessened by its four-hour transit over Florida. Leaving Florida, Andrew reached the Gulf of Mexico. Once there, Andrew was fueled by warm Gulf waters that whipped up the hurricane's winds to 140 mph.

In the north-central Gulf of Mexico, currents of air steered Hurricane Andrew into a more sparsely populated section of the south-central Louisiana coast, dotted with bayous and marshlands.

Shortly after its landfall near Morgan City, Louisiana, Andrew rapidly weakened. Its strength depleted, the once terrifying hurricane reclaimed its status as a "tropical storm," producing heavy rain in its last hours of existence. Local flooding was touched off as rainfall totals in excess of seven inches were recorded in Louisiana and Mississippi.

On August 27, as if wishing to hold onto its reign of terror, Andrew stirred up several damaging tornadoes. By midday on August 28, Andrew began to merge with weather patterns over the mid-Atlantic states.

Within hours, the sky reclaimed the energies that had composed Hurricane Andrew, the third-strongest storm ever to strike the United States and the most devastating hurricane to race across American territory in 25 years.

In just two weeks—from its birth to its demise—Hurricane Andrew left behind a trail of devastation and death, and years of rebuilding at a cost of many billions of dollars. ■

Humidity

Humidity is the amount of dampness in the air. Although you can't see it, all air holds a certain amount of dampness in the form of water vapor. It is this vapor that collects on blades of grass in the early morning or on the inside of your window on cold winter nights. And it is this vapor that, under the right conditions, becomes fog, rain, hail, snow, or any other form of precipitation.

But where does water vapor come from in the first place? Most of the water vapor becomes airborne through evaporation from bodies of water around the globe. We know that when the sun shines on a body of water, the water absorbs heat energy. This heat causes molecules of water to evaporate, rise, and become part of the air.

Most evaporation takes place around the equator, the area receiving the greatest amount of solar energy. The ocean is the principal source of this moisture. In fact, billions of kilograms of water evaporate from the surface of the ocean every day. Once water has entered the atmosphere in the form of water vapor, its molecules become much more active than when they were liquid. Their vibrating motion is really energy stored up in the molecules. It is called *latent*, or hidden, heat.

As water continues to evaporate into the atmosphere, the humidity of the air increases. But air at any given temperature can store only so much water. When air reaches a point where it can hold no more water, it is said to be saturated. When the temperature increases, the atmosphere can hold more water vapor, but if the air becomes cooled, the excess water condenses in the form of water droplets.

The temperature at which this condensation occurs is called the *dew point*. The dew point will vary according to how much water vapor is in the air. Water-laden air may form drops of dew at 65 degrees Fahrenheit, but much drier air may hold its small amount of humidity in suspension until the temperature reaches 32 degrees.

People are often interested in knowing just how humid it is. This is commonly expressed in the form of relative humidity, a ratio of the amount of water vapor in the air compared with the amount the air can hold at a particular temperature. For example, if a meteorologist speaks of 90 percent relative humidity, you know that the air is at 90 percent of the total amount of water vapor it can hold. Relative humidity changes as moisture enters and leaves a given mass of air. It will also change if the temperature changes, because warmer air can absorb more moisture and cooler air less.

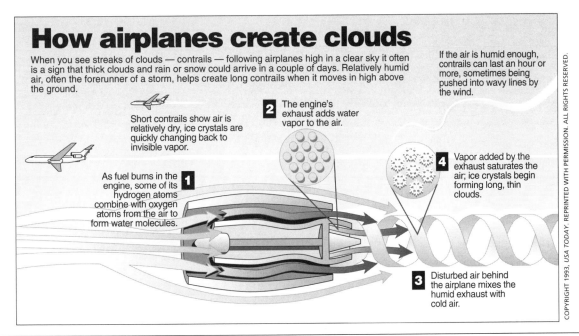

How airplanes create clouds

When you see streaks of clouds — contrails — following airplanes high in a clear sky it often is a sign that thick clouds and rain or snow could arrive in a couple of days. Relatively humid air, often the forerunner of a storm, helps create long contrails when it moves in high above the ground.

Short contrails show air is relatively dry, ice crystals are quickly changing back to invisible vapor.

If the air is humid enough, contrails can last an hour or more, sometimes being pushed into wavy lines by the wind.

2 The engine's exhaust adds water vapor to the air.

1 As fuel burns in the engine, some of its hydrogen atoms combine with oxygen atoms from the air to form water molecules.

4 Vapor added by the exhaust saturates the air; ice crystals begin forming long, thin clouds.

3 Disturbed air behind the airplane mixes the humid exhaust with cold air.

Meteorologist

NANCY COBB
NATIONAL OCEANIC &
ATMOSPHERIC
ADMINISTRATION
SILVER SPRING, MD

I am a meteorologist who helps other meteorologists with their writing. I'm sort of a translator of science into everyday English.

I got my interest in meteorology from my dad. He was always taking me out fishing or sailing. He would watch the sky and tell me just by looking at the clouds what was going to happen. I was impressed by that, so I got interested in looking at clouds too. The summer before my senior year in high school, I decided I was going to be a meteorologist.

My typical day consists of writing at my computer and spending a lot of time on the phone talking to scientists. By talking with them, I get a better understanding of what they do so that I can explain it to people who don't understand science.

Scientists in some of our laboratories in Colorado developed a theory to explain why the ozone hole over Antarctica is forming. So I knew what was going on before a lot of other people did. I like being on the cutting-edge of research in the field of atmospheric science.

To become a meteorologist, you should definitely focus on math. When I was in school, I took math all the way through my four years of high school. I wish I could have taken more.

Take algebra, trigonometry, and calculus. This will give you a good background for going on to more advanced areas of math. If you have the chance, take physical science, earth science, and physics.

Chaos is a new area of math that I find fascinating. Chaos theory was developed by a meteorologist. It has a lot to do with how far in advance we can make an accurate forecast. We have been treating the atmosphere as if its processes were linear, but they are not. Atmospheric processes are very irregular. You don't know where that butterfly is going to land next or which volcano is going to erupt and when. We don't understand all the variables and probably never will.

I'm sort of the NOAA coordinator for information about the atmospheric effects of the eruption of Mt. Pinatubo. I put out a report every month based on information I gather from other scientists throughout the agency. Some of our scientists

have detected a definite cooling trend since Mt. Pinatubo erupted. Someone at NASA has done a computer model which simulates the atmosphere, and came up with the prediction that we will be getting cooler for maybe two or three years and then we will slowly start to recover until temperatures are normal again.

It's kind of interesting that we are getting this cooling on top of the predicted global warming everybody has been talking about. Global warming is very hard to detect, and having this cooling blip on top of it will make it more difficult to determine what's going on.

In the seventies and early eighties, hurricanes were very destructive. They hit the coast of the United States frequently. Then during the middle eighties, hurricanes started taking different tracks. They were staying out in the ocean instead of hitting land. During that time people became complacent about hurricanes. We now think that hurricanes go in cycles. After the lull in the mid-eighties, we may be entering the part of the cycle where we will have more hurricanes hitting the coast.

Hurricane Formation

Hurricanes, from a West Indian word for "big wind," are one of the most powerful and frightening storms we know. From time immemorial, they have wreaked havoc and destruction along their paths as they made their way through the tropics and subtropics.

The months of June through November are usually considered "hurricane season" in the United States. Each year, an average of six hurricanes form in the tropical areas of the Atlantic Ocean. A newly formed tropical storm usually moves westward, sometimes picking up enough speed and intensity of wind and rain to be labeled a hurricane. They then often follow a northward course until landfall, creating tidal waves and floods along the coastline.

Under what conditions do hurricanes come to be? Several factors must be present for a hurricane to form. The first ingredient is a vast stretch of open sea that has been heated by the sun beaming down from a nearly cloudless sky. Indeed, in order to spawn a hurricane, the temperature of the sea must be at least 80 degrees. The heated sea fills the air above it with moisture. The water vapor rises and eventually condenses to form clouds.

Hot moist air, though necessary, is not sufficient for hurricane formation. A low-pressure area associated with the prevailing subtropical winds of the North Atlantic must trigger a hurricane into motion, causing the hot moist air to slowly spin toward a center, which is to become the calm eye of the storm. As it spins, the air rises, moisture condenses, heat is thrown off, and additional clouds are formed. As the warm air begins to rise, the system resembles a chimney as it carries away the heat of a roaring fire. The hotter the fire, the greater the draft up the chimney. The hotter the ocean surface, the greater the upward flow of air in the center of a forming hurricane.

Once born, a hurricane careens over the ocean like a top, picking up moisture and energy as it goes. If it hits land, it dumps its cargo of rain and cuts a swath of destruction up to several hundred miles wide. If the destruction is great enough its name is retired, never to be used again. If it misses land, it usually dies out when cooler northern waters rob it of its sustaining energy.

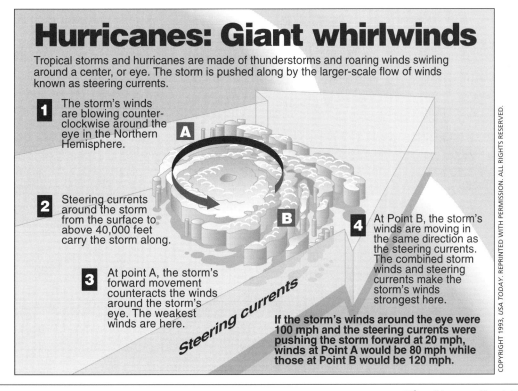

Hurricanes: Giant whirlwinds

Tropical storms and hurricanes are made of thunderstorms and roaring winds swirling around a center, or eye. The storm is pushed along by the larger-scale flow of winds known as steering currents.

1 The storm's winds are blowing counter-clockwise around the eye in the Northern Hemisphere.

2 Steering currents around the storm from the surface to above 40,000 feet carry the storm along.

3 At point A, the storm's forward movement counteracts the winds around the storm's eye. The weakest winds are here.

4 At Point B, the storm's winds are moving in the same direction as the steering currents. The combined storm winds and steering currents make the storm's winds strongest here.

Steering currents

If the storm's winds around the eye were 100 mph and the steering currents were pushing the storm forward at 20 mph, winds at Point A would be 80 mph while those at Point B would be 120 mph.

Tracking a Hurricane

Purpose
To track a hurricane and use other weather features to predict its path.

Materials
- Hurricane tracking map (page 22)
- United States weather maps (supplied as needed)

Procedure
Background: As a hurricane expert, you are often called on to track approaching hurricanes and alert the public about possible threats. If there is a possibility that a coastal area under your jurisdiction will be hit by a hurricane in 24 to 36 hours, it is your job to issue a *hurricane watch*. A *hurricane warning* is issued when hurricane winds are likely to hit land in 24 hours or less. When a hurricane warning is issued, immediate actions for protection of life and property must begin. These actions include boarding up windows, evacuating low-lying areas, and setting up shelters. Since these actions can be extremely costly for urban areas, hurricane experts are careful not to issue warnings too early. However, they must not issue warnings too late!

You are responsible for issuing watches and warnings for Charleston, South Carolina. You have been tracking an approaching storm for the past seven days. The table below shows the path of this eighth hurricane of the season. Since this storm could threaten Charleston, you decide to plot its path on a hurricane tracking map. You number each day and indicate A.M. or P.M. as you plot each position. You also connect the dots with a dashed line when the maximum wind speed is between 51–119 km/hr (tropical storm), and with a solid line if the maximum speed is 120 km/hr or more (hurricane).

Analyze the path of the storm for days numbered one through seven and predict where and when the hurricane will hit the United States' mainland. Consult with the other members of your team to reach a consensus prediction to share with the class. Issue hurricane watches or warnings for the appropriate coastal areas as necessary. Tracking data for day eight and a United States weather map for that day will be available after you make your prediction.

Repeat the process through landfall, checking and revising your prediction and issuing or canceling watches or warnings. Be ready to discuss and answer questions during a "debriefing session" after the hurricane has moved inland.

Hurricane Tracking Data					
Day	Time (EST)	Latitude (°N)	Longitude (°W)	Max. Wind Spd. (km/hr)	Forward Spd. (km/hr)
1	7:00 A.M.	13	27	59	33.4
	7:00 P.M.	12.5	31		34.8
2	7:00 A.M.	12.5	34.5		32.4
	7:00 P.M.	12.5	38	92	31.1
3	7:00 A.M.	13	41.5		27.5
	7:00 P.M.	13	44.5		25.2
4	7:00 A.M.	13	47.5	98	17.6
	7:00 P.M.	14	50.5		6.6
5	7:00 A.M.	14	53	136	13.1
	7:00 P.M.	15	56		20.9
6	7:00 A.M.	15.5	58	125	20.7
	7:00 P.M.	16	60.5		18.2
7	7:00 A.M.	16.5	62.5		9.9
	7:00 P.M.	17	64	160	9.5

Questions to consider in the debriefing session

1. Did the hurricane form where most other hurricanes form? Explain.

2. Why did this hurricane move from east to west through the first seven days? Explain in terms of earth wind patterns.

3. On day seven, the forward speed of the hurricane slowed markedly. Look carefully at your map and suggest a reason why the storm slowed down.

4. How did the United States weather map influence your prediction on day eight?

5. How did your hurricane watch area change after day eight? Did you have to change the warning area before the storm hit land? If so, try to explain why you changed the area.

6. What weather features over the United States mainland were most important in steering this hurricane as it moved inland?

Conclusions

You have been asked to appear on *Good Morning America* to explain the factors that were most helpful to you in predicting the destructive path of the hurricane. Since you will have only one minute to give your answer, you decide to mention two factors and then explain the more important one.

Write notes for yourself. Be sure to list two factors that helped you predict the path and explain why one of the two seems to be a better predictor.

Copy additional data here.

Day	Time (EST)	Latitude (°N)	Longitude (°W)	Max. Wind Spd. (km/hr)	Forward Spd. (km/hr)

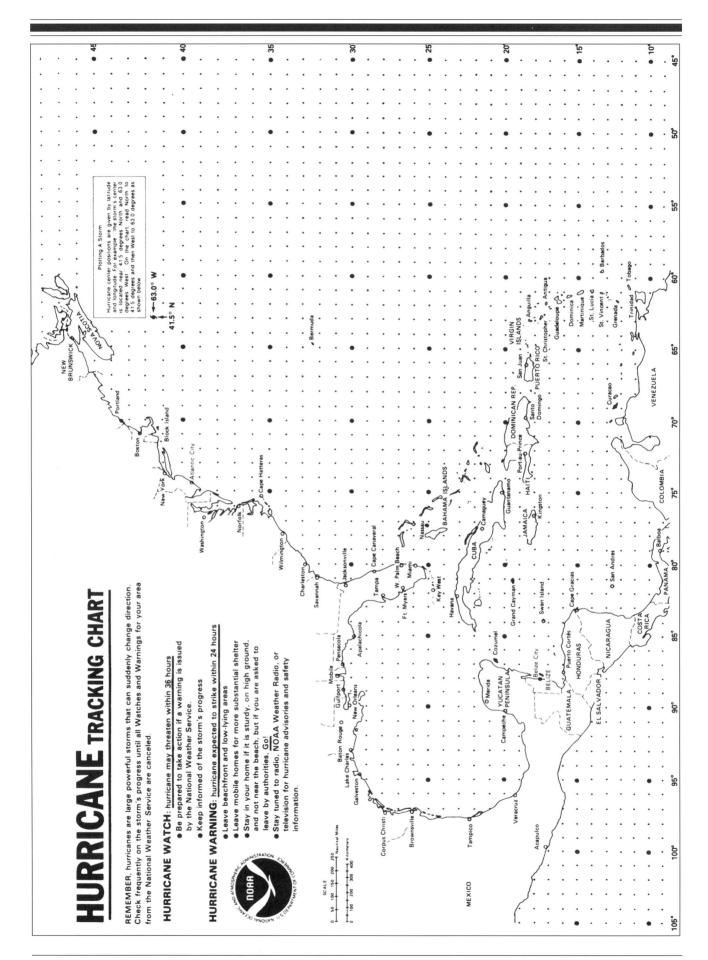

HURRICANE TRACKING CHART

REMEMBER: hurricanes are large powerful storms that can suddenly change direction. Check frequently on the storm's progress until all Watches and Warnings for your area from the National Weather Service are canceled.

HURRICANE WATCH: hurricane may threaten within **36 hours**.
- Be prepared to take action if a warning is issued by the National Weather Service.
- Keep informed of the storm's progress.

HURRICANE WARNING: hurricane expected to strike within **24 hours**.
- Leave beachfront and low-lying areas.
- Leave mobile homes for more substantial shelter
- Stay in your home if it is sturdy, on high ground, and not near the beach, but if you are asked to leave by authorities, Go!
- Stay tuned to radio, NOAA Weather Radio, or television for hurricane advisories and safety information.

Plotting A Storm

Hurricane center positions are given by latitude and longitude. For example, the storm's center is located near 41.5 degrees North and 63.0 degrees West. On the chart, read North to 41.5 degrees and then West to 63.0 degrees as shown below.

→ 63.0° W
41.5° N

SCALE

Hurricane Preparedness

Forecasters do not issue hurricane warnings unless the prediction of where the storm will make landfall has the highest probability of being accurate.

The reasons for needing such an accurate forecast are many. A typical hurricane warning, say for a 300-mile stretch of property along the Gulf of Mexico, could cost upwards of $50 million as people close offices, board up homes, or shut down manufacturing plants. An inaccurate forecast, therefore, could be economically devastating to cities in terms of lost business and disruption of services. Moreover, if a forecast is given that later proves wrong, it could make it all the more difficult for people to accept future warnings. You could call it the "cry hurricane" phenomenon.

On the other hand, forecasters must make a prediction of where a hurricane will first touch land far enough ahead of time for those threatened to evacuate in an orderly way.

When a hurricane watch is in effect, a hurricane may make landfall within 24–36 hours. You should be prepared to take action if a hurricane watch is issued. Hurricane safety rules during a watch include:
- Listen to local officials
- Check often for official bulletins on radio, TV, or National Oceanic and Atmospheric Weather Radio
- Fuel your car
- Moor small boats or move them to safe shelter

- Check mobile home tie-downs
- Stock up on canned food
- Check radio and flashlight batteries
- Tape, board, or shutter windows to prevent shattering
- Wedge sliding glass doors to prevent lifting from their tracks

When a hurricane warning is issued, a hurricane is expected to strike in 24 hours or less. Action to protect life and property should begin immediately. Key things to remember during a hurricane warning are:
- Obey local officials
- Stay tuned to radio and TV for official bulletins
- Move valuables to upper floors
- Board up garage and porch doors
- Fill containers with a several-day supply of drinking water. (Your bathtub can hold water for flushing the toilet.)
- Turn up your refrigerator to maximum cold and don't open unless necessary
- Use phones for emergencies only
- Stay indoors on the downwind side of your house, away from windows

Hurricanes produce great *storm surges,* domes of water that come sweeping across the coastline, near the area where the eye of the hurricane makes landfall. You should leave areas that might be affected by a storm tide or stream flooding. Before leaving your home, shut off the water and electricity. Take only small valuables and important papers—travel light. Lock up your house and drive carefully to the nearest designated shelter using recommended evacuation routes. Since designated shelters can only accommodate about 10 percent of the population and are usually not comfortable places to ride out a storm, it is recommended that shelter be sought with friends and relatives in a well-stocked, safe building in a nearby community.

The lady's house next door had no roof. When we went to dig her out there was nothing in her house that wasn't soaked or broken. She and her two children had stayed in a closet that was being held together by one piece of wood.

LEANDRO ONOFRIO
KENDALL, FL

Hurricane Specialist

DR. FRANK MARKS JR.
NOAA/AOML
MIAMI, FL

I became interested in meteorology when I was a sixth grader in New York. I was delivering newspapers to a guy who had strange things on his roof. It turned out that he was a science teacher and a weather nut. He had meteorological devices all over his roof. The more we talked, the more interested in weather I became. In high school we had a big meteorology program where I would plot weather maps and do forecasts. I had so much fun, I decided I wanted to be a weather forecaster. While in college working on my bachelor's degree in meteorology, I learned that there is a lot more to weather than just plotting symbols on a map and making forecasts. I learned that if you want to understand how weather works, you must learn the laws of the atmosphere. I became interested enough in learning those laws that I went on to graduate school.

In graduate school, I found out that physics and math are extremely important in understanding meteorology. I had to work hard to catch up on those subjects. I knew a lot about meteorology, but not a lot about math and physics.

Communication skills are extremely important too. Knowledge is only gained when it is shared by a large group of people so that they can build on that knowledge. Communication is not only writing, it is organizing your thoughts into a coherent flow of ideas and then presenting them verbally or in written form.

My typical day is pretty dry. I usually come in, sit at my computer, check my electronic mail, then I spend a lot of time looking at data from my past flights and experiments. I spend a good half of my day writing. Another third of the day I am working on the computer, looking at data, analyzing the data, and trying to organize my thoughts.

In hurricane season (August, September, and October), we travel for three or four weeks. To do my experiments, I fly into hurricanes. In the past twelve

years, I have flown into twenty-five hurricanes or tropical storms. I have flown into the eye of a hurricane about two hundred times. On September 15, 1989, I was on a P3 flight into Hurricane Hugo. We were at 1500 feet when we went into the storm. We came in on the weak side, but when we hit the eye-wall, we hit winds of over 160 mph and very vigorous turbulence, three up/down drafts exceeding 40 mph in rapid succession. We lost an engine, due to mechanical problems, and dropped to about 800 feet above the roiling surface. It was frightening! It made me realize that, no matter how much you do this type of work, Mother Nature has more surprises than we know about. You can never take things for granted.

What I like best about my work is that every time I do something, I learn something new. I like the challenge of trying to figure out how things work. Of course, things never work the way you expect them to. Something breaks or doesn't work at all. Also, Mother Nature is never the same twice. When you're flying an airplane at 250 mph, things change dramatically and rapidly. You have to have a simple plan that you can execute no matter what happens. It's not an easy task, but it is a challenge every time.

For the past three months, I have been in Guadalcanal, one of the Solomon Islands. We are part of a big international program in the Solomon Islands related to air/sea interaction. That part of the South Pacific is the warmest ocean in the world. It's a major area for storm formation. Things like El Niño originate there.

I contracted malaria the last few weeks I was in Guadalcanal. Malaria is a disease caused by a parasite carried by mosquitoes. You can't inoculate yourself against it. You can only take a preventative, usually a quinine-based drug. The strain of malaria I contracted is new, so now I am the subject of a medical study. The Center for Disease Control in Atlanta wants to study my blood.

Your team is charged with warning the public about where a storm is going to hit. That's a real problem! When Andrew hit us, I lost a window and a lot of trees. Three miles farther south, houses were destroyed. When a storm is 200 miles offshore, you can't predict where it will hit land with much accuracy. I would take two approaches in dealing with the uncertainties of issuing a warning. First, I would overwarn, and second, I would stress preparedness. Over-warning is costly, but if you can save a life, I think it's worth it. Property damage is going to happen no matter what. The only way to deal with property damage is proper insurance and preparedness. You cannot over-prepare. Preparedness is one of our major allies in this business because of the fact that, even if we could predict perfectly, we can't stop the damage from happening.

Daily Weather Maps

Purpose
To follow the movement of weather across the United States in order to make a prediction.

Materials
- Daily weather map from a local newspaper
- Two outline maps of the United States

Procedure
Background: As a reporter for a newspaper in a coastal town, you have just been told that when the newspaper's weather forecaster goes on vacation you will be the one who forecasts the weekend weather. The person who now makes the forecasts tells you that the best way to predict the weather is to follow weather systems as they move across the United States.

You have only five days to track the motion of low- and high-pressure systems and fronts, then you must use whatever knowledge you've gained to predict the weekend weather. The paper's forecaster has suggested the following steps:

1. Obtain the weather map from your local paper each day.
2. Record daily weather information in an organized way. Make sure you record anything that might help you make your prediction, such as the position and movement of pressure systems and fronts, daily high and low temperatures, cloud cover, precipitation, and so forth. Record anything that you and your team decide may be helpful in predicting the weekend weather. (A collection of the maps themselves might be helpful.)
3. After you have completed collecting information from the daily maps, you are ready to make a prediction of the weekend weather. Using two outline maps of the United States, indicate where you think pressure systems and fronts will be located for Saturday and Sunday. Prepare a weather prediction for your adopted community for each day.
4. Save the actual weekend weather maps so that you can compare them with your predictions. Also, complete an actual weather table for Saturday and Sunday, including high and low temperatures, cloud cover, and precipitation.
5. Display your prediction maps and the actual weather maps on a poster. Attach a booklet containing your supporting research.

Questions to think about as you proceed
1. According to the weather maps, is precipitation generally associated with high- or low-pressure systems?
2. In what general direction does weather move across the United States?
3. What causes weather to move in this direction?

Where Do Hurricanes Form?

Purpose
To determine the best location for scientific instruments designed to detect hurricanes as they form.

Materials
- Hurricane tracking map (see page 22)
- Hurricane origin data-table

Procedure
Background: You and your partner are part of a research team working for the National Oceanic and Atmospheric Administration (NOAA). Your job is to put out a large number of floating instrument platforms to study the weather and ocean conditions that lead to the formation of hurricanes. But first you must choose the best possible location for these instruments. The area must be no larger than five degrees latitude by five degrees longitude.

You have already gathered ten years of data on where hurricanes are "born." You and your partner decided to define "born" as the place where hurricanes first became tropical storms and were given a name. You are each ready to plot hurricane origins on a hurricane tracking map.

The resulting map is like a scatter plot. Use this visual display of hurricane origins to determine where to place the instrument platforms.

Conclusions
As you choose the area where the platforms will be released, think of several reasons for your choice. Mark the site on a hurricane tracking map and be prepared to present your decision and reasons to the class.

Hurricane Origins 1982–1991								
Year	Lat (°N)	Long (°W)	Year	Lat (°N)	Long (°W)	Year	Lat (°N)	Long (°W)
1982	23	85	1986	30	78		17	23
	14	24		27	89		11	25
	27	94		32	78		13	27
	23	72		11	56		12	53
	27	68		23	52		20	93
1983	27	92		24	63		21	84
	27	76	1987	27	94	1990	11	57
	32	63		29	76		29	75
	30	73		15	26		16	33
1984	13	55		24	40		17	83
	15	45		11	25		39	28
	39	65		11	56		9	53
	28	78		16	82		13	50
	15	26	1988	42	69		15	40
	28	60		29	89		10	32
	25	77		21	96		19	34
	25	72		35	54		16	59
	17	67		24	89		31	56
1985	31	66		27	80		23	82
	27	83		15	62		22	62
	34	74		13	34	1991	36	71
	24	87		12	56		27	76
	22	78		11	47		27	56
	26	67		16	82		10	35
	15	28	1989	27	96		29	53
	35	74		18	48		20	84
	18	69		24	91		31	67
	24	93		17	48		36	70
	22	64		18	32			

Natural Hazards Planner

**WILLIS E. BROTHERS
NORTH CAROLINA
DIVISION OF EMERGENCY
MANAGEMENT**

Today I am working on a presentation for the Legislative Research Commission here in North Carolina. I am preparing a briefing of the incidents of all the natural hazards of North Carolina, by county and by legislative district. My typical day is kind of a hodgepodge of all the hazards we have that affect North Carolina: hurricanes, earthquakes, flash floods, and tornadoes.

North Carolina is a tornado-prone state as well as hurricane-prone state. In fact, the number of incidents of tornadoes has increased in North Carolina by a factor of three over the last twenty years. North Carolina is kind of unique. According to the Hurricane Center, it is the most hurricane-prone state. We're concerned that if you take a storm like Andrew or Hugo and bring it across our coast, we will see some storm-surge heights in the neighborhood of 23 to 25 feet. Working with the Army Corps of Engineers and tax assessors in four counties, we figured that almost all of the cottages and beach homes in a 75 to 80 mile stretch would be wiped out. We have already briefed the Legislative Research Committee on this and we've used it for a FEMA project that is involved with catastrophic events. Three years ago we were

fortunate enough to receive the National Hurricane Award for the most pro-active emergency-preparedness hurricane program of the seventeen coastal states.

What I like about my job is that I find something new and different every day. I work with representatives from counties and other states that are in the same situation we are. A typical day could include anything from a meeting with somebody from FEMA, to a meeting with county people, to a meeting with one of the legislative study groups, to just sitting at my computer working on a project.

To prepare for this type of work, it is helpful to know a little about meteorology. But the main thing you need to know is what local government can and can't do. You need to know the relationship between local, state,

and federal government. You need to have a feel for emergency planning, and an idea of emergency medical services. It helps to have knowledge of law enforcement; a background in insurance is helpful too. You need a little knowledge about engineering and construction (how buildings are put together), utilities (infrastructure, lifelines, communications), and an understanding of earth sciences. In college, I majored in public administration.

Regarding water purification and contamination following a hurricane, contamination is inevitable. To make sure people have safe water after the storm, they should store it in the bathtub or buy gallon jugs of water from their local stores. We recommend a three-day supply of drinking water. People normally do this when a warning is issued.

Different Kinds of Precipitation

Fog

Fog. How many mystery and horror stories depend upon its wispy nature?

Like a cloud on the ground, fog is created when there is little wind and humid air is cooled to its dew point. At the dew point, water vapor begins to condense into tiny droplets.

Fog will burn off as the sun rises in the morning. The sun's warmth raises the temperature above the dew point and the fog evaporates.

Rain

As you likely know, clouds are formed from the water that evaporates from the seas, lakes, rivers, humid land masses, and vegetation. Even sweaty joggers out for their daily runs make their contributions. Millions of tiny water droplets form a cloud when this evaporated water condenses around salt, dust, and other particles in the air.

Why does this condensation occur high in the sky most of the time? It's because, just as with fog formation, cloud formation begins when the dew point is reached.

And, as air rises it expands and cools.

Which do you think must rise higher before a cloud forms, dry air or moist air?

In order for rain, snow, sleet, or hail to start falling from the clouds, some of the droplets must increase in size a million times or more. In the case of warm rain clouds—clouds whose tops are warmer than 0 degrees C (32 degrees F)—droplets may grow by bumping into each other inside the cloud. As they grow, they eventually become too heavy to remain suspended in the air and they fall to the ground.

In cold clouds, with tops well below freezing, water vapor condenses to form ice crystals. Ice crystals grow quickly, and as they fall through the cloud, they collect other droplets and smaller crystals along the way. Eventually, these ice crystals will reach the ground as raindrops, snowflakes, or a mixture of rain, snow, or sleet.

Small raindrops make for a light form of rain called *drizzle*. They measure less than .05 centimeters (.02 inches) across and can take as much as an hour or more to reach the ground. Light rain generally falls from a layered cloud not more than two or three kilometers (a mile or two) thick. In contrast, a heavy, sudden shower of large raindrops usually falls from a cloud 14 kilometers (9 miles) or more deep.

Sleet

Drops of water falling from the sky, freezing as they plummet downward through colder air near the ground, can form sleet. Sleet is made of small drops of water that freeze into pellets of ice, usually smaller than 0.8 centimeters (0.3 inches) in diameter. As frozen raindrops, sleet is generally mixed with liquid drops.

The gentle rattling on windowpanes caused by sleet is often an early warning sound of an impending ice storm. As sleet continues to fall, layers of the icy material can build up on power lines and tree limbs, snapping them when they can no longer take the added weight of the ice. Roads can turn into something like skating rinks—too dangerous to drive over—when covered with sleet.

Hail

When lumps of ice fall from thunderclouds, we experience hail. Golf-ball-sized hailstones are common in certain areas. In fact, the largest hailstone on record fell on September 3, 1979, in Kansas, and had a circumference of 44.5 centimeters (17.5 inches). But hail is usually pea-sized and falls in short, intense showers called *hailstorms*.

Hailstones are formed when water droplets freeze into small ice crystals in a thundercloud. Strong air currents in the thundercloud toss the pieces of ice up and down between the cold and warmer parts of the cloud. Every time the hailstone enters a

After the hurricane, my family and I had to move out of the only home we've ever known. I didn't want to move. I didn't want new friends. Moving scared me. My family didn't know where we would go. We were homeless.

This experience has broadened my outlook on life. I don't think so much about material things anymore, because they can be gone in an instant. Family, support, and love—knowing that they're always there and will always love you is what really matters.

LEAH KOSSEFF
MIAMI, FL

warmer area, moisture sticks to its surface. Each time the air current lifts it back into the colder part of the cloud it freezes solid again. This way the hailstone gains several coats of ice as it is whisked up and down between the colder and warmer

parts of the cloud. Finally, it grows too heavy to remain up in the cloud and falls to earth.

Snow

When billions of tiny ice crystals cluster together and fall from cold clouds, we have snow. The crystals are formed when the water vapor freezes directly onto dust particles in the atmosphere without becoming water droplets first. For this to happen, the upper atmosphere must be very cold, generally around –20 degrees C (–4 degrees F). Snow crystals grow as more ice is deposited on them. All snow crystals have six sides, but their shapes depend on how much moisture is in the air and how cold it is. Since these conditions vary greatly within a cloud, no two snowflakes are exactly alike.

You have probably noticed how sometimes snow is large and fluffy and perfect for making snowballs, while at other times it is fine and powdery. Large, fluffy, wet snowflakes generally fall at temperatures just around freezing, because the freezing crystals stick together. Light fluffy snow takes up much more space than an equal amount of rain. In fact, since air can occupy so much space within fallen snow, a fresh layer of cold snow may be up to 36 times as deep as the same amount of rainwater.

The Barometer

One of the great scientific innovations of the Renaissance was the mercury barometer, invented in 1643 by Evangelista Torricelli, one of Galileo's assistants. Today's mercury barometer has changed little since the days of Torricelli.

Torricelli took a tube closed at one end, filled it with mercury, and placed it open-end-down in a dish of mercury. Air pressure on the mercury in the container kept the mercury from flowing back down into the dish. And as the air pressure increased, it would press down harder on the mercury in the dish, forcing it up into the tube. A ruler attached to the tube was used to measure the height of the mercury. Extremely high pressure at the surface can push the mercury up to about 32 inches in the tube.

A barometer is probably the most useful instrument for forecasting weather. As the barometric pressure drops, you will know that low pressure, and a likelihood of rain, are in the forecast. A rise in air pressure brings the promise of good weather.

The unit of metric measurement of atmospheric pressure is the *millibar*. One millibar is equal to the pressure of 1/32 inch of mercury. At sea level, the pressure is usually about 1,013 millibars. According to several barometers in Homestead, Florida, when Hurricane Andrew passed over, the atmospheric pressure measured only 926 millibars. The lower the barometric pressure, the stronger the storm.

30"

Mercury

Mostly I remember sitting on the stairs saying that I was very sleepy. My feet were getting very cold because the wind was going through the windows. I thought the house was going to blow up because of the pressure.

My dad was downstairs trying to blockade the windows with mom's mattress. When it got to be too strong for him, he came to the stairs with us. My mom was calming us down, saying that everything was going to be fine, that we were going to be okay.

After the hurricane, it was like a bomb had hit.

When we came back to our house, I found that I was allergic to the mildew in the walls. It was all over the place. For one day and night I was sneezing from asthma, and I was very uncomfortable. The doctor said I had to stay out until they repaired the house.

FRANK ROSA
RICHMOND HEIGHTS, FL

Pathway of Destruction

Hurricane Andrew killed a total of sixty-two people as it swept through the Bahamas and slammed into Florida and Louisiana. The swath of damage was about 50 miles wide. In hard-hit Florida, Andrew's incredible power reduced 25,524 homes to rubble, damaged 101,241 others, and left an estimated 250,000 people homeless. Southern Dade County looked like a war zone. At the height of the storm, three million homes and businesses in Florida were without power and thrown into darkness. The current estimate of damage is about $25 billion.

In comparison, two other hurricanes that have hit the United States demonstrate the sheer damage caused by Andrew:

- In 1969, Hurricane Camille slammed into the Mississippi coast killing 256 people, destroying more than 5,500 homes, with another 12,500 residences suffering major damage. Upwards of 700 businesses were demolished or significantly damaged, leaving almost $4 billion in damage.

- Hurricane Hugo tore through the Virgin Islands and Puerto Rico in 1989 prior to hitting the Carolinas, causing $5.9 billion in damage and taking the lives of eighty-five people.

Hurricane Andrew eliminated nearly all basic services in a number of areas. After Andrew passed,

STUDENT VOICES

After the hurricane, we built a fire in the backyard for warmth because we had no electricity for a week. My neighbors would come over and we would sit in a circle and talk about it. We had been friends with our neighbors before the hurricane. After the hurricane we helped each other.

BRITTANY GORBY
KENDALL, FL

the immediate concern of disaster-management teams was the spread of diseases. Lack of clean water could cause diarrhea, an illness that is communicable and would spread quickly if fresh water were not immediately made available. Also, without proper toilet facilities, large numbers of people would be exposed to untreated human waste, a condition that might spark an increase in tuberculosis cases. Tuberculosis is a serious lung disease.

The search for missing people was more frustrating. Digging through neighborhoods in ruin, crews combed through the hurricane wreckage with power tools and construction equipment to remove fallen walls and roofs. Search dogs were brought in to locate the injured and dead. A Goodyear blimp was pressed into service, flashing messages to those people without radio or television.

The reminders of Hurricane Andrew's power—broken sidewalks, destroyed roofs and house frames, fallen trees, and broken glass—had to be carted off to Florida landfills already brimming with debris caused by previous hurricanes. In Florida alone, the zone of devastation extended 15 miles inland and 22 miles north-to-south.

The environmental reshaping of storm-ravaged parts of Florida, including the 1.4 million-acre Everglades National Park, was yet another worry. Millions of native palms, hardwood trees, and evergreens were flattened by the hurricane. Scientists

➤ continued on page 32

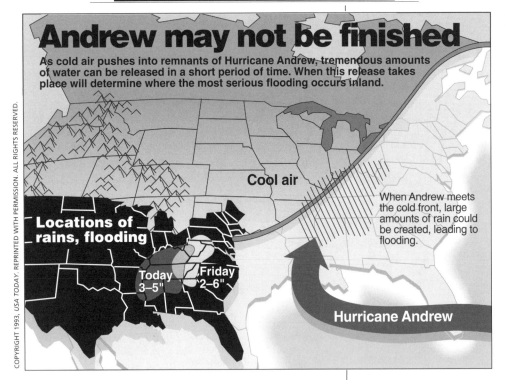

Andrew may not be finished

As cold air pushes into remnants of Hurricane Andrew, tremendous amounts of water can be released in a short period of time. When this release takes place will determine where the most serious flooding occurs inland.

Cool air

Locations of rains, flooding

Today 3–5"

Friday 2–6"

When Andrew meets the cold front, large amounts of rain could be created, leading to flooding.

Hurricane Andrew

➤ continued from page 31

fear that this native vegetation may be overtaken by fast-growing species brought in from outside the area, foreign vegetation that has already secured an ecological foothold elsewhere along the Florida peninsula. Similarly, the Everglades may have been affected by seeds from exotic plants and trees blown into the park by the hurricane. If true, this environmentally sensitive area, located just west of coastal cities destroyed by Andrew, may see a shift in its ecology in future years.

The storm also left many agricultural areas destroyed or damaged. Approximately 80 percent of Dade County's 3,655 farms, which produce 90 percent of all limes sold in the United States, were lost. Other tropical orchards with crops such as mangoes and papayas were also destroyed.

Animal populations suffered as much as humans. Three hundred rare southeast Asian birds were missing from Miami's Metrozoo after Andrew. Volunteer rescue teams searched for injured and starving dogs, cats, cows, and horses.

Louisiana fishermen are also expecting to see long-term effects, courtesy of Hurricane Andrew. As the storm pushed across the Louisiana coastline, that state's system of canals, lakes, and bayous was whipped up. Sediments in the bottom of the waterways were churned up, suffocating at least 182

million freshwater fish, according to one count. That loss was valued at $160 million by local fishing businesses. Additionally, about $3.5 million of Louisiana's $30 million annual oyster harvest was lost to the storm's ferocity.

The destructive impact of Hurricane Andrew required nearly thirty thousand Army, Navy, Air Force, Marine Corps, and National Guard personnel to help in day-to-day support and cleanup operations. The military quickly mobilized units to provide stricken hurricane victims with needed food, water purification, sanitation, medical care, and engineering skills. They also set up enough tents to house the thousands of people needing shelter.

The mega-disaster response was coordinated by the Federal Emergency Management Agency (FEMA), responsible for synchronizing the relief efforts of twenty-seven federal agencies. FEMA was criticized, however, for its perceived slowness in responding to the natural disaster. Some blamed the slow response on state officials who were slow to call for federal assistance. On September 18, Congress approved a record $11.1 billion disaster relief package to assist not only Hurricane Andrew victims, but also to aid those suffering from Hurricane Iniki and Typhoon Omar. Typhoon Omar blasted Guam on August 28, while on September 11, Hurricane Iniki ravaged Kauai in the Hawaiian Islands—back-to-back disasters of epic proportions.

In the aftermath of Hurricane Andrew, in the Bahamas, Florida, and Louisiana, the task of rebuilding slowly began. But in that rebuilding many questions were raised about construction techniques necessary to make the dwellings hurricane resistant. Mobile homes that were not properly anchored to the ground were easy targets for the hurricane. But why were so many houses destroyed?

Many older cinder-block houses survived. But many houses constructed during the building boom of the 1980s didn't. It seems that rapid growth in south Florida's population led to the use of shoddy materials and poor workmanship as some developers took shortcuts in their construction for greater profits.

Oddly, Dade County's tough building codes require homes to be able to withstand a minimum of 120 mph winds. But evidence in the rubble pointed to the fact that builders had not adhered to this law. Shortcuts taken during construction led to the horrific loss of so many South Florida homes. The situation was compounded by inadequate building inspections, with reports that many inspectors were bribed by construction firms to overlook regulations.

From small beginnings, large and powerful hurricanes can grow. Each displays its own personality, leaving behind its individual signature of destruction. Hurricane Andrew became the costliest storm in United States history, displaying an awesome power to destroy homes, businesses, vegetation, and lives.

Those who survived its fury will long remember the monster from the tropics—the killer storm called Hurricane Andrew. ■

Lucky dog

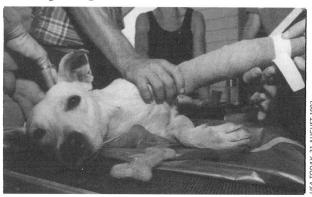

USA TODAY, 31 AUGUST 1992

By David Bergman, AP

HELPING HAND: Volunteers at a special clinic in Perrine, Fla., put a cast on Miss Thing, a hurricane victim.

ANIMAL RESCUE: Teams of veterinarians and volunteers spread out in vans and a helicopter to rescue starving dogs, cats, cows and horses, many of which were maimed or killed in Hurricane Andrew. About 100 riders saddled up to search for about 500 lost horses in Dade County. "This is incredibly sad," said volunteer Cornelia Perez. "We've found horses and cattle that were impaled on trees." Scores of stray animals have wandered the debris-strewn streets south of Miami surviving on contaminated water and food bits found in rubble. Most Humane Society shelters are operating without power and water and are reporting an overload of pets brought in by owners who couldn't care for their furry friends following Andrew.

Environment took a beating
Still, 'it could've been worse'

By Linda Kanamine
USA TODAY

Hurricane Andrew trampled the Sunshine State's scenic environmental landmarks, felling thousands of tropical trees in Miami and tearing up the world-famous Everglades.

And in Louisiana, it left 7 million dead fish in oxygen-depleted waterways. Hardest hit: Atchafalaya Basin in south central Lousiana.

"But the bottom line is, we're greatly relieved because the situation could've been considerably worse," says John Ruddell of Florida's Department of Environmental Regulation.

Still, the storm's 160-mph gusts left a heavy mark as they whipped through an already fragile ecosystem:

▶ Divers have found destroyed coral and sponge formations off Miami.

▶ Sunken boats in bayside marinas leak fuel.

▶ Winds and water may have wiped out nesting sites of crocodiles in Florida and Biscayne bays.

But the most visible damage is in the 1.4-million acre Everglades National Park, haven to a dozen endangered species.

Estimated damage to the park: $27 million.

"Rows and rows and rows of trees are down," says Jim Coleman, National Park Service regional director in Atlanta.

Coleman also says there is concern that the park might not be able to recover. "This storm, 400 to 500 years ago, would've been no problem, the place would've bounced back," he says.

The Everglades is eerily quiet without its usual population of wading birds, whose tree island nests and rookeries have been wiped out. Coleman says as much as 50% of the park's pine trees may be lost, as well as much of the hardwood hammocks and other timber.

That's particularly bad news as the hardier melaleuca trees — considered a water-guzzling foreign pest species — may take over. Another danger: downed trees could present a future fire danger.

The good news: 24 endangered Florida panthers that wear radio tracking collars and roam Big Cypress Swamp and the Everglades survived the storm, Coleman says.

Biologists now are concerned that their main food source — white-tailed deer — did not survive the storm.

What havoc Andrew didn't cause directly could come in its aftermath: Florida Gov. Lawton Chiles has approved open burning of solid waste and debris in 12 burn pits.

"That could leave smoke in the air around here for months," says Jim Webb of The Wilderness Society.

Experts also expressed concern that fires of junked building material could spew asbestos, a once-common insulation material that was banned in 1978 because of its cancer risk.

"These are extraordinary circumstances," says Environmental Protection Agency's Hagan Thompson. "If emissions were way out of bounds, burning would be curtailed."

USA TODAY, 2 SEPTEMBER 1992

Contractors sweep into south Florida

'The idea that we're working off somebody else's hardship is depressing'

By Martha T. Moore
USA TODAY

CUTLER RIDGE, Fla. — Last year, David DelSol shut down his Miami engineering and contracting business, laying off 19 people he just couldn't keep working in the slumping south Florida economy. Now he's on top of a house on Franjo Road, rebuilding a roof ripped away by Hurricane Andrew. He has a crew of six, needs more employees and has more work than he can handle. "Look around," he says. "Even if you've got a couple of states' worth of contractors working, there's enough for six months."

Or six years. Hurricane Andrew destroyed 63,000 homes and countless businesses and damaged thousands more Aug. 24. Already, Dade County is turning into one big construction site. The roads are full of pickups loaded with ladders and rolls of roofing materials. On trees and telephone poles — those that are still standing — hang handwritten signs advertising tree cutting, roof patching or just "Rebuilder." And on roofs — those houses that still have them — contractors sweltering in 90-degree heat are laying down plywood and tar paper.

A state Department of Labor economist estimates that the devastation could create up to 7,000 construction jobs — as many as Dade County lost the past two years. For contractors, the recession is over. And builders from all over the USA want a piece of the action.

"We're getting calls from vultures all over the world," says Chuck Lennon of the Builders Association of South Florida. "They're circling."

Then again, there's a lot of work to do. Right now, it's mostly clearing trees, patching roofs to make them watertight — known as "drying in" a house — and cleaning up debris. Homeowners in the hardest-hit areas are still worrying about food, water and shelter. But in less-damaged neighborhoods, rehabbing has begun.

Mike Adair drove down from Palm Beach with his partner, Rocky Elson, to stuff local mailboxes with business cards. "I can't sleep at night with the opportunities going through my head," Adair says. Meanwhile, his Bobcat bull-

USA TODAY, 4 SEPTEMBER 1992

By Gaston de Cardenas, AP

HURRICANE HELP: Navy personnel unload lumber from the USS Sierra in Miami on Monday as part of a massive federal relief effort. Three more ships are expected to dock today.

dozer has been clearing fallen trees in wealthy Coconut Grove for $45 an hour. Peter Casanas came from New York to repair two rental properties and picked up six more reconstruction jobs. "We've had offers left and right," says Casanas, who is commuting to South Dade from Key Largo, 40 miles away.

Randy Blair came from Orlando, one of a 14-man roofing crew that arrived with 5,000 rolls of tar paper. Doing business as Disaster Dry In Team, they get $1,500 to patch a roof. It takes about two hours. "You don't have to look (for jobs)," he says. "People just come up and ask you." He says he'll make "an easy grand a week."

Builders are arriving with plans to stay months or longer. "We plan on possibly two years," says Bob LaRose, a contractor from DeLand, north of Orlando. He wants to buy four or five badly damaged homes — he's seen signs advertising houses for sale for $1,000 — repair them, house his crews there until work runs out, then resell.

Many of the new arrivals are disaster specialists. They went to South Carolina after Hurricane Hugo in 1989. Inrecon, a Dearborn, Mich.-based company that specializes in insurance reconstruction, has brought in 300 workers and $750,000 worth of building materials from its offices across the country. Inrecon's tactic: concentrate the work in a few expensive housing developments. In Cutler Grove, an upscale development in Cutler Ridge where Inrecon has parked an air-conditioned trailer office, the company signed up 31 of 83 homes at a homeowners' association meeting. "We go anywhere there's a disaster," says Vice President George Fenton. "This is our forte."

Blaine Byars of Columbia, S.C., says the same thing. He and two friends drove down in a pickup loaded with five rolls of plastic, 20 sheets of plywood and generators and chainsaws to sell on consignment from a pawnshop, "and we were in business." Unemployed for three months at home, he plans to stay in south Florida permanently. Now he's parked on the side of the road opposite the Old Cutler Shopping Center with his merchandise spread out, a spray-painted "Low Prices" sign and one of his partners asleep in the shade of the truck.

"We're guessing there'll be more work than contractors for at least 12 to 18 months," he says. So far, he's had the best luck in wealthy neighborhoods, patching two houses with plywood and boarding up windows. He got $1,200 at each house. "Those people want their houses built today, and they've got the money to pay up front," he says.

Up the road, Todd Rishel and Tracy Gorczyca sit in lawn chairs behind the Winnebago parked on the grass verge. "I've worked three hurricanes" — David in 1979, Hugo and now Andrew, says Rishel. In South Carolina, he made $33,000 in 2½ months. Here, he figures, he can make $2,000 on a good day cutting and hauling damaged trees.

The influx of builders doesn't necessarily annoy local contractors, though they are quick to point out that out-of-towners may not be familiar with south Florida's building codes. "There'll be work for everybody," says Robert Lennon, working on clearing debris at Old Cutler Shopping Center.

The work is plentiful but not easy. Dade County has suspended requirements for building permits for emergency repairs. But building supplies can be scarce, and prices are going up — from $7.50 a sheet for plywood to $13 at MCR Lumber in Naranja, which is operating in the open since its buildings were flattened by Andrew. To get workers, LaRose had to raise wages paid laborers to $10.50 an hour from $8. He's paying skilled workers $18 an hour, up from $13. Crews are sleeping in motor homes, in campgrounds, with friends. LaRose spent one night sleeping atop his U-Haul. A few food trucks have appeared, but there are no 7-Elevens nearby to fetch a cold drink when the sun gets blistering.

"I told my guys, 'Be prepared for the worst — bring your own water, coffee, lunch, whatever,'" says DelSol. "It's like a war zone out there."

However badly needed the jobs, the construction industry is in the uncomfortable position of profiting from the misfortune wrought by Andrew. Worried about their collective reputation, the south Florida home builders, with help from the National Association of Homebuilders, are preparing TV ads to run next week giving tips on how to avoid getting ripped off. Local media have already hammered home the message: Don't hire a contractor who doesn't have a license, including a certificate of competency, and insurance. And don't hand over any money up front.

"The idea that we're working off somebody else's hardship is depressing," says Ron McGlennon of Avalon Construction in Fort Lauderdale, which is importing 45 men from an Ohio construction company. TV doesn't do justice to the devastation, he says. "You have to see it and hear it and smell it. It tears your heart out."

But the cold reality remains. Paul Reinke cut short a vacation in Puerto Rico to fly to Miami after Andrew hit. A crew of 11 men from his Thunder and Lightning Demolition, based in Brooksville, 50 miles north of Tampa, met him here. A week later, they are ripping the roof off a Kmart in the Old Cutler Shopping Center. They have orders from insurance companies to raze 187 houses. He did the same in South Carolina after Hugo.

"I hate to come to these places. But you gotta work," he says. "Ninety percent of us come down to get the money. There might be 10% who are here to help. The rest of us are here for the bucks."

Contributing: Bill Montague

Hidden construction faults

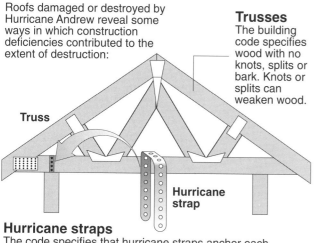

Roofs damaged or destroyed by Hurricane Andrew reveal some ways in which construction deficiencies contributed to the extent of destruction:

Trusses
The building code specifies wood with no knots, splits or bark. Knots or splits can weaken wood.

Truss

Hurricane strap

Hurricane straps
The code specifies that hurricane straps anchor each crossbeam or truss to the wall.
Problem: Inadequate straps or wrongly installed straps can let the wind push trusses and the roof off a home.

Reading a Weather Map: Highs, Lows, and Fronts

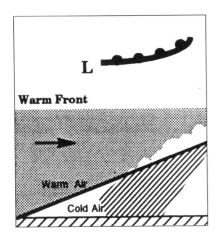

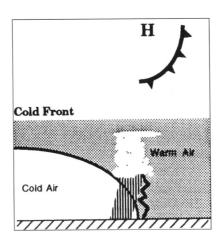

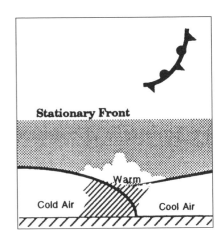

Constructing a weather map that can accurately forecast weather across the U.S. takes a cast of thousands. Meteorologists need millions of observations from weather stations, weather ships, satellites, balloons, and radar that every minute are making detailed recordings of temperature, pressure, wind direction, and other relevant measurements.

The data they gather are entered into the Global Telecommunications System (GTS), which relays it to powerful supercomputers that assemble a comprehensive picture of atmospheric conditions around the world. From these maps, computers are able to create forecasts up to seven days in advance.

Weather Map Symbols

Newspaper weather maps are easy to understand if you know the definitions of a few meteorological terms and what the symbols represent.

Highs and Lows

High- and low-atmospheric (air) pressure areas are represented by an "H" or "L" in the center of a black circle. Lines that join points with the same air pressure are called *isobars*. Newspaper weather maps usually do not show isobars; instead they often show isotherms. *Isotherms* are lines that connect points with the same temperature.

Pressure systems "drive" the world's weather, so forecasting our future weather is dependent upon locating ridges of high pressure and troughs of low pressure.

Fronts

The air around us is constantly being either warmed or cooled by the surfaces over which it travels. At any given time, there are large masses of the atmosphere that are either warm or cold. When these warm and cold air masses bump into each other, a boundary called a *front* is formed. When the warm air is

pushing through, the boundary is called a *warm front*. A *cold front* indicates that the cold air mass is pushing its way through. And a standoff between the two air masses is called a *stationary front*.

It is along these fronts that dramatic and sometimes violent weather occurs. The mixing of cold and warm air causes clouds to form along the front and produce rain. Fronts often travel very fast. When a cold front passes through your town, a period of showers can quickly be followed by a bright sunny day. The effect of a warm front lasts longer. As it approaches, clouds slowly increase. Then the rain begins and lasts for several hours.

Cold fronts are usually indicated on a weather map as lines with triangles pointing out from the line. The symbol for warm fronts is a line with semicircles dotting it. Stationary fronts have alternating triangles and semicircles.

Up, Up, and Away

Purpose

To investigate how quickly different surfaces heat up and how this affects the air above them.

Materials

- Surface samples
- Heat lamp and support (ring stand)
- Containers to hold samples (for example, beaker for water)
- One thermometer

Procedure

Background: You and a friend recently visited a small airport and noticed a group of people preparing gliders for takeoff. As you watched the gliders being moved onto the runway and the cables from the tow planes being attached to them, you asked your friend, "How long can gliders stay in the air?" A pilot standing nearby told you that it depends on how well the pilots use thermals. Thermals are updrafts of warm air. He said, "You need to know how to use what's on the ground in order to stay in the air." He claimed that some surface features produce stronger thermals because they heat up faster and get hotter than other surface features. Some of the surfaces he mentioned are bodies of water, parking lots, grass- and tree-covered areas like golf courses and farms, and open areas that have very little vegetation.

After watching a few takeoffs and landings, you and your friend decide that this is something you've got to try. However, before you actually take off and

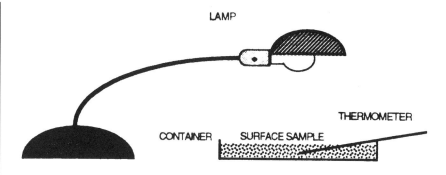

fly, you plan on doing a little work in the science lab to determine which surfaces will produce the strongest thermals.

You'll need to

1. Find items that you can use in the lab to represent the different surfaces you'll be gliding over—buildings, water, grass-covered fields, plowed fields, and so on.
2. Design an experiment that will test how the surfaces are heated.
3. Design your experiment so that all samples are tested under the same conditions. (As you know, this is called controlling variables.) On a sheet of notebook paper, write your lab procedures so that someone could use them to check your work. BE CAREFUL WHEN USING THE LAMP. IT MAY GET VERY HOT.
4. Decide how you will collect temperature data and make a table for recording it.
5. Organize your findings in a way that allows you to rank the surfaces from best to worst when it comes to getting the longest glider flight.

Conclusion

Now that you've completed your research, you're ready to analyze the data to determine which surfaces heat up the most and therefore produce the best thermals. Use your results to rank the surfaces in order from best to worst.

The Hydrologic Cycle

Water is in constant motion. If we were able to follow a single water molecule over the course of several days we might see it change state and location many times. The cycle water goes through is called the *hydrologic cycle.*

Let's imagine one way a water molecule could travel in this cycle. (You can think of many other ways to complete this cycle.) A single molecule on the surface of a lake near your home absorbs energy from the sun. The energy of heat is transformed into energy of motion, causing the molecule to move about rapidly. When it gains enough speed, it *evaporates,* leaving the surface of the lake to join other energetic water molecules in an invisible gaseous state we call *water vapor.*

The molecule, carried high into the atmosphere by updrafts of warmed air, begins to lose energy. Energy loss results from expansion of the air as it climbs higher and higher. When enough energy has been lost the *dew point* will be reached and the air will become *saturated.* This molecule and others condense around a dust particle in the air, forming a droplet of water. As more droplets form and gather together, a visible cloud forms. This cloud becomes dense enough for *precipitation* to fall. Precipitation might be liquid (rain) or solid (sleet, snow, or hail).

The single molecule we've focused on—along with millions of other molecules—is now part of a raindrop. This raindrop lands on a roof, one of the thousands of drops falling in a light shower.

The drops run together in a trickle. Trickles merge as they flow down the roof, into the gutter, and onto the ground below. Some water molecules soak into the soil. They will sink deeper until they join the underground reservoir called *ground water.* Our molecule does not soak into the soil but instead it flows along the ground until it reaches a creek near your home. From there it flows with trillions of other water molecules on a trip that ends in one of the oceans.

At any point along the way the water molecule may begin the hydrologic cycle again. All it needs is enough energy to evaporate.

Can you think of how the hydrologic cycle provides a continuous supply of fresh water for us to drink?

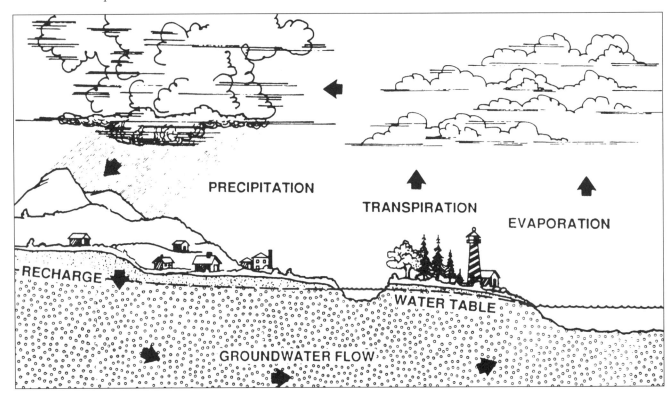

PRECIPITATION

TRANSPIRATION

EVAPORATION

RECHARGE

WATER TABLE

GROUNDWATER FLOW

Local Moisture

Purpose
To explain everyday, ground-level examples of the water cycle.

Materials
- Blank, lined paper
- Tape

Procedure
Background: Your newspaper has a tradition known as the Friday Challenge. It began in 1954 when the paper's founder, Andy Hugo, decided that not only should a newspaper report the news, it should also help to educate the community. The Friday Challenge strategy is to print a series of articles on a selected topic in the Monday through Thursday editions, then on Friday challenge readers to apply what they have learned to new and different situations.

This week's features have been about the water cycle. Topics included evaporation, condensation, dew point, cloud formation, and precipitation. The Friday Challenge this week brings the water cycle closer to home, challenging readers to explain everyday occurrences in terms of the water cycle.

Each week the editor has teams try out items for the Friday Challenge before they are published.

Have each member of your task team write one of the following moisture event statements on the top of a piece of notebook paper. Now take two or three minutes to write an explanation of the event at the very bottom of the paper, mak-

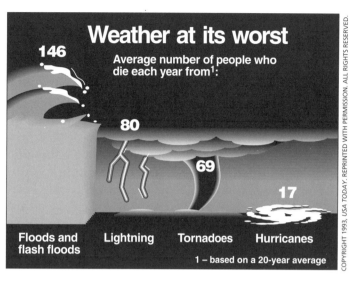

Weather at its worst

Average number of people who die each year from[1]:

146 — Floods and flash floods
80 — Lightning
69 — Tornadoes
17 — Hurricanes

1 – based on a 20-year average

ing sure to tell why the event happened. At a signal, fold your explanation under so no one can see it, then pass the paper to the person on your right so that they can add their explanation. You will add your explanation to a sheet coming from your left. This process continues until all papers have three or four explanations.

When you have finished writing, have the person holding each paper read the statements. Try to agree on one statement that does the best job of explaining each event. Your teacher will select your best explanation for one of the events to be read to the class.

Following this reporting and discussion, your teacher will give each of you a statement describing an event involving moisture. It will be similar to the ones you have been dealing with together. You will have to write your own explanation of that new event.

Moisture Events
- "After you take a shower, the bathroom mirror is fogged."
- "You open the freezer door on a hot summer day. A cloud quickly forms and falls toward the floor. When you close the door, the cloud disappears."
- "It is a cold winter day. You are wearing glasses. When you walk in from the cold to a hot, crowded room, your glasses fog up."
- "You are exercising vigorously outside on a cold day. You are wearing glasses. Suddenly, your glasses begin to fog up."
- "It is a very hot afternoon. It clouds up and rains for only a short time. Then the sun comes out again. The road surface on your street begins to steam."
- "It is a winter evening and it has just snowed a few inches. You're looking forward to a snow day. Then the temperature rises a few degrees, the snow begins to melt, and fog begins to form."

Reporter

HECTOR F. GARZA-TREJO
BROWNSVILLE, TX

I work for *The Brownsville Herald*. My official title is Health and Environment Reporter. I'm also editor of our Spanish newspaper, *El Heraldo de Brownsville*.

My job can be divided in two parts, gathering information and writing the final story. Gathering information requires deciding what the topic of my next story will be, contacting people who know about that topic, taking notes, and organizing the most important facts. Writing the story means putting down in simple words the information I found about the topic I chose.

Being a journalist has given me the opportunity to go places where few people can go, while doing something I love to do—storytelling.

The newspaper I work for is an afternoon newspaper. I must be at my office at 7:30 A.M. I usually spend the first hour and a half organizing my notes and getting last-minute information for that day's story. I need to write fast after that. Daily stories must be ready by 10 or 10:30. Then I spend the afternoon gathering information for a story for the following morning.

The most interesting thing about my profession is being able to tell readers what's going on in a part of the world they can't see. Meeting prominent people and going to unusual places makes my job very interesting, too.

I need to know a little bit of everything, or at least have the willingness to learn quickly. As my paper's health and environment reporter, I've learned a lot about biology, medicine, physics, and other sciences. Writing stories about hurricanes has prompted me to learn a bit about oceans and the atmosphere, even about planes and balloons. Perhaps the best advice I can give students is to not see learning as a taxing obligation. See it as a step you must take to understand the world around you, and to open doors to interesting careers.

To become a journalist, you must develop good language skills by reading about all kinds of subjects and writing in every possible style. Read every book you can—fiction books, police stories, historical novels, science-fiction books, and political accounts. Then try writing about anything in any form you can—reports, essays, short stories, long stories, fictional narratives, or anything else you'd like to try. After reading and writing for a while, you will see that understanding things seems easier, and telling other people about them is fun.

STUDENT VOICES

I was at camp in the mountains of Pennsylvania during the hurricane. When I got back to my neighborhood, it looked so different. All the familiar landmarks were gone. There used to be a really big tree for climbing in my front yard, but the hurricane knocked it over and my father had someone pull it out. I never thought it could be this bad. I was happy to see my baseball cards were okay though.

Now my friends are far away, and I don't go to the same school anymore. I don't have a back yard for my dog. I don't have a basketball court. Now we are living in an apartment complex. It's harder to communicate with my friends because now it's a long distance call.

ALEX KOSSEFF
MIAMI, FL

Hurricane Hunters Take to the Sky

You may not think of your local TV weather forecaster as a brave superhero, but some of the meteorologists at NOAA—the National Oceanic and Atmospheric Administration—and from the United States Air Force, could be considered among the most daring people in the world.

These weather experts, in their quest to learn more about hurricanes and to provide information to forecasters and the public, fly into hurricanes in an attempt to measure a hurricane's force and better predict the impact it will have on us earthlings.

These "hurricane hunters" monitor the hurricane's winds, air pressure, temperature, and the storm's exact location. The information they gather is combined with data acquired from geostationary weather satellites 22,300 miles above the equator that keep an eye on the hurricane's location and size. The data are fed to supercomputers that assist meteorologists in issuing frequent forecasts.

Shortly after Hurricane Andrew's wild winds had passed over Florida, NASA's aeronautics division was called upon to give a quick-response assessment of the hurricane damage to assist relief efforts. NASA dispatched one of its research planes—a specially-equipped Lear jet.

In addition to photographic images, the scientists also used a special scanner to take digital images that could be plugged into computers for post-Andrew analysis and planning.

Three weeks after Andrew ravaged Florida, Hurricane Iniki devastated the Hawaiian island of Kauai. NASA's flying scientists were again requested to survey the damage to Kauai.

Utilizing NASA's high-flying ER-2 research plane, meteorologists employed five different types of cameras to aid in the assessment. Their high-resolution camera is capable of detecting an object about six-feet long from an altitude of 60,000 feet.

The many images were valuable in looking at access routes to damaged areas, evaluating farming problems like flooding, and planning cleanup procedures.

Environmental Scientist

STEVE HOCKING
FEDERAL ENERGY
REGULATORY COMMISSION
(FERC)

My real title is Environmental Protection Specialist. I work for the Office of Hydropower Licensing (OHL) within the Federal Energy Regulatory Commission (FERC). As an Environmental Protection Specialist, my job is to ensure that environmental concerns are considered and protected during the construction and operation of hydroelectric projects. The issues that concern me include a project's impact on wetlands, wildlife, soil erosion, and stream flow.

I became interested in ecology and environmental protection when I worked at a nature center when I was thirteen, and later when I worked as an intern at the National Aquarium in Baltimore. I have always enjoyed the study of wildlife and natural resources.

Most of my time is spent reviewing and evaluating proposals to protect environmental resources. Proposals are submitted by project owners and reviewed by agencies like the United States Fish and Wildlife Service and the State Department of Fish and Game.

The most interesting thing I have done is to assist in efforts to develop a bald eagle management plan.

In my work, I use my knowledge of environmental science, ecology, botany, and natural resources management. Much of my work also involves writing.

When you are looking for solutions to environmental problems, look at the big picture first. Then break down the situation into smaller individual problems, and finally, concentrate on your top priority.

Disaster's lessons
Damage greater than experts expected

By Dennis Cauchon
USA TODAY

Wind experts are befuddled by why Hurricane Andrew did so much property damage.

Most homes in the hurricane's path were designed to handle the sort of wind gusts that blew in with Andrew — or so the experts thought.

"There's far more damage than I would have expected for that type of storm," says Kishor Mehta of the Wind Engineering Research Center at Texas Tech University. "Obviously, we don't know as much as we thought about wind damage."

Water — not wind — usually does the worst damage in a hurricane. Not this time.

Tough building codes put into place over the last 20 years were expected to prevent such widespread devastation.

Most Florida and Louisiana building codes require that homes withstand 110 mph winds. Hard-hit Dade and Broward counties have a 120 mph requirement. That includes gusts of 140 mph, like those from Andrew.

Single family homes always are most vulnerable because wind pressure is concentrated on a small space. But they should have held up better.

"We have to figure out if the problem was not good enough building codes, a lack of enforcement or whether Hurricane Andrew was more powerful at ground level than we thought," says Palm Beach County building code official Dominick Sims.

Sims suspects the storm's power is to blame. He says people's ears popped as if they were on an airplane, indicating the pressure at ground level was extremely strong.

"The storm behaved more like something from *The Exorcist* than a hurricane," he says.

Southern Building Congress chief executive William Tangye says many homes did not meet code. Buildings designed by engineers — trained in wind damage — fared well, he says. But many builders don't know how to translate a 110 mph requirement into practice.

"What does 110 mph mean in practice — use a 1-by-6 or a 1-by-8, 50 nails or 100 nails?" says Tangye, whose group sets building codes.

Doing everything right can add 2% to 4% to the cost of a house, Tangye says. The key: fastening every part — roof, top plate, etc. — firmly.

"A house is a series of fragile connections," says Tangye, a structural engineer. Connections, not building material, are the weak point, he says.

Entire trailer parks are now empty fields. Some mobile homes landed blocks away.

Florida requires mobile homes to be linked to the ground with a 4-foot anchor. But most still have 2-foot anchors — not good enough in Florida's sandy soil.

"Homes with 4-foot anchors did as well as conventional homes," says Orville Cummings, assistant director of Florida's Bureau of Mobile Home Construction.

Fewer than 5% of houses in Dade and Broward counties are mobile homes, but most were in the hardest hit area.

Mehta says the massive damage may be the result of engineering ignorance.

The USA does not have a wind tunnel that accurately simulates how winds damage a low-rise building. "Oddly, we know less about what wind does to a one- or two-story building than what it does to a 50-story building," Mehta says.

Contributing: Linda Kanamine

USA TODAY, 28–30 AUGUST 1992

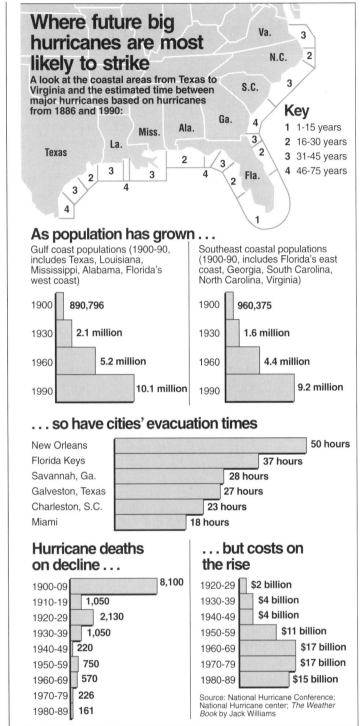

Where future big hurricanes are most likely to strike

A look at the coastal areas from Texas to Virginia and the estimated time between major hurricanes based on hurricanes from 1886 and 1990:

Key
1 1-15 years
2 16-30 years
3 31-45 years
4 46-75 years

As population has grown . . .

Gulf coast populations (1900-90, includes Texas, Louisiana, Mississippi, Alabama, Florida's west coast)

Year	Population
1900	890,796
1930	2.1 million
1960	5.2 million
1990	10.1 million

Southeast coastal populations (1900-90, includes Florida's east coast, Georgia, South Carolina, North Carolina, Virginia)

Year	Population
1900	960,375
1930	1.6 million
1960	4.4 million
1990	9.2 million

. . . so have cities' evacuation times

New Orleans	50 hours
Florida Keys	37 hours
Savannah, Ga.	28 hours
Galveston, Texas	27 hours
Charleston, S.C.	23 hours
Miami	18 hours

Hurricane deaths on decline . . .

Years	Deaths
1900-09	8,100
1910-19	1,050
1920-29	2,130
1930-39	1,050
1940-49	220
1950-59	750
1960-69	570
1970-79	226
1980-89	161

. . . but costs on the rise

Years	Cost
1920-29	$2 billion
1930-39	$4 billion
1940-49	$4 billion
1950-59	$11 billion
1960-69	$17 billion
1970-79	$17 billion
1980-89	$15 billion

Source: National Hurricane Conference; National Hurricane center; *The Weather Book* by Jack Williams

Agency labors amid disaster and criticism

Says staffer about FEMA: It has 'good soldiers and and crummy generals'

By Judy Keen
and Paul Hoversten
USA TODAY

The federal government has a pact with disaster victims: When calamity strikes, it rushes in with all its resources to help rebuild their lives.

But in the aftermath of Hurricane Andrew — and other recent disasters — many say the Federal Emergency Management Agency, the government's first line of crisis assistance, has failed to fulfill that contract.

As Andrew's survivors scramble to supply their basic needs — food, water, medicine, a dry place to sleep — fingers again are pointing, as they did after 1989's Hurricane Hugo and San Francisco earthquake, at FEMA.

"It's a disgrace, a national disgrace that our country doesn't have a better system of providing immediate, much-

By Anne Ryan, USA TODAY

HOME: A tent city in Homestead, Fla., set up by Marines from Camp Lejeune, N.C., is almost ready for occupancy.

needed response and assistance in the wake of huge natural disasters," says Mayor Joseph Riley of Charleston, S.C., which took the brunt of Hugo's punch.

USA TODAY, 1 SEPTEMBER 1992

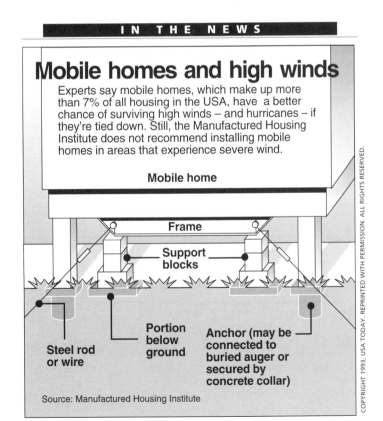

Mobile homes and high winds

Experts say mobile homes, which make up more than 7% of all housing in the USA, have a better chance of surviving high winds – and hurricanes – if they're tied down. Still, the Manufactured Housing Institute does not recommend installing mobile homes in areas that experience severe wind.

Mobile home

Frame

Support blocks

Steel rod or wire

Portion below ground

Anchor (may be connected to buried auger or secured by concrete collar)

Source: Manufactured Housing Institute

COPYRIGHT 1993, USA TODAY. REPRINTED WITH PERMISSION. ALL RIGHTS RESERVED.

The Story—Part 3   **43**

The Naming of Hurricanes

Why Hurricanes Are Named

Experience shows that the use of short, distinctive given names in written as well as in spoken communications is quicker and less subject to error than the older more cumbersome latitude-longitude identification methods. These advantages are especially important in exchanging detailed storm information between hundreds of widely scattered stations, airports, coastal bases, and ships at sea.

The use of easily remembered names greatly reduces confusion when two or more tropical storms occur at the same time. For example, one hurricane can be moving slowly westward in the Gulf of Mexico, while at exactly the same time another hurricane can be moving rapidly northward along the Atlantic coast. In the past, confusion and false rumors have arisen when storm advisories broadcast from one radio station were mistaken for warnings concerning an entirely different storm located hundreds of miles away.

History of Hurricane Names

For several hundred years many hurricanes in the West Indies were named after the particular saint's day on which the hurricane occurred. Ivan R. Tannehill describes in his book *Hurricanes* the major tropical storms of recorded history and mentions many hurricanes named after saints. For example, there was Hurricane Santa Ana which struck Puerto Rico with exceptional violence on July 26, 1825, and San Felipe (the first) and San Felipe (the second) which hit Puerto Rico on September 13 in both 1876 and 1928.

Tannehill also tells of Clement Wragge, an Australian meteorologist who began giving women's names to tropical

---

We spent the storm in a shelter. When we went back to our house, I was crying because I didn't even recognize it. I didn't even recognize my neighborhood. My father was crying too. That was the first time I had ever seen my father cry. The roads were muddy and disgusting. All the poles were down. We didn't even know if we were in the right place.

When we went to our house it was scary because the front of the house was ruined. The roof was torn off, the door had blown right in. It was really weird; some of our neighbor's furniture was in our house.

ANGELINA DIAZ
HOMESTEAD, FL

storms before the end of the nineteenth century.

An early example of the use of a woman's name for a storm was in the novel *Storm* by George R. Stewart, published in 1941, and later made into a film by Disney. During World War II this practice became widespread in weather map discussions among forecasters, especially Air Force and Navy meteorologists who plotted the movements of storms over the wide expanses of the Pacific Ocean.

In 1953, the United States abandoned as confusing a two-year-old plan to name storms by a phonetic alphabet (Able, Baker, Charlie) when a new, international phonetic alphabet was introduced. That year, this nation's weather services began using female names for storms.

The practice of naming hurricanes solely after women came to an end in 1978 when men's and women's names were included in the Eastern North Pacific storm lists. In 1979, male and female names were included in lists for the Atlantic and Gulf of Mexico.

EXCERPTED FROM "THE NAMING OF HURRICANES," U.S. DEPARTMENT OF COMMERCE, NOAA-NATIONAL WEATHER SERVICE

List of Names for Atlantic Storms

1994	1995	1996
Alberto	Allison	Arthur
Beryl	Barry	Bertha
Chris	Chantal	Cesar
Debby	Dean	Diana
Ernesto	Erin	Edouard
Florence	Felix	Fran
Gordon	Gabrielle	Gustav
Helene	Humberto	Hortense
Isaac	Iris	Isidore
Joyce	Jerry	Josephine
Keith	Karen	Klaus
Leslie	Luis	Lili
Michael	Marilyn	Marco
Nadine	Noel	Nana
Oscar	Opal	Omar
Patty	Pablo	Paloma
Rafael	Roxanne	Rene
Sandy	Sebastien	Sally
Tony	Tanya	Teddy
Valerie	Van	Vicky
William	Wendy	Wilfred

List of Names for Eastern Pacific Storms

1994	1995	1996	1997
Aletia	Adolph	Alma	Andrea
Bud	Barbara	Boris	Blanca
Carlotta	Cosme	Cristina	Carlos
Daniel	Dalila	Douglas	Dolores
Emilia	Erick	Ellen	Enrique
Fabio	Flossie	Fausto	Felicia
Gilma	Gil	Genevieve	Guillermo
Hector	Henriette	Hernan	Hilda
Ileana	Ismael	Iselle	Ignacio
John	Juliette	Julio	Jimena
Kristy	Kiko	Kenna	Kevin
Lane	Lorena	Lowell	Linda
Miriam	Manuel	Marie	Marty
Norman	Narda	Norbert	Nora
Olivia	Octave	Odile	Olaf
Paul	Priscilla	Polo	Pauline
Rosa	Raymond	Rachel	Rick
Sergio	Sonia	Simon	Sandra
Tara	Tico	Trudy	Terry
Vicente	Velma	Vance	Vivian
Willa	Wallis	Winnie	Waldo
Xavier	Xina	Xavier	Xina
Yolanda	York	Yolanda	York
Zeke	Zelda	Zeke	Zelda

If over 24 tropical cyclones occur in a year, then the Greek alphabet will be used following Zeke or Zelda. Names of particular individuals have not been chosen for inclusion in the list of hurricane names.

English: Writing a Business Letter

Directions

Complete the writing activity below. Be sure to read the prompt carefully.

Prompt

As a member of your newspaper staff, you need to gather information on the city in which your newspaper is published. Write a business letter to the chamber of commerce of your city explaining the type of information you need and requesting that they send it to you as soon as possible. You should not ask for information about hurricanes.

Before you begin writing, brainstorm the kinds of information your group will need to complete your city's newspaper. Think about how you can explain your needs to the chamber of commerce. Keep in mind that you will need to write your request in correct business-letter format.

Now write a business letter to the chamber of commerce of your city in which you explain your task and request information.

As you write this letter, you will want to do the following:

- First, as a group, develop a plan for gathering information on your city. Think about what you will want to learn.
- Then use a pre-writing strategy such as listing or webbing to organize your ideas.
- Next, think about how you will want to word your request so that the chamber of commerce is most likely to respond quickly.
- Research the correct format for a business letter.
- Use these ideas and this information to collaboratively write a rough draft.

- Using the rubric for informative writing given to you by your teacher, collaborate on evaluating your draft.
- Now, revise your work taking into consideration the responses given during the group evaluation.
- Look over your collaborative work. Proofread, using the Proofreading Guidesheet on page 51, and the correct business-letter format.
- Prepare a final copy of the group's letter, keeping in mind that business letters are expected to have no spelling, punctuation, or grammatical errors.
- Prepare an envelope to mail your letter. Be sure the zip code is correct.

English: Writing a Scene

Directions

Imagine the conversation that might take place between the mayor of your city and the producer of the local television station's nightly news regarding the imminent dangers of the approaching hurricane. Write a dramatic scene in which these two characters weigh the merits of telling the public all the information while at the same time reassuring people so as not to incite panic.

Make sure the characters, dialogue, and plot are believable, based on the information that you have already learned. Be sure to keep in mind the ethical issues of journalism that might influence the decision on how much information to give the public, and how to most safely communicate that information.

English: Reading in Response

Directions

Read "The Wind," another lyric or narrative response to a storm event. Explain how these personal responses differ from the expository descriptions of storms that appear in news reports. Write your own poetic or narrative response to a hurricane or other serious storm that you have experienced.

The Wind
by James Stephens

> The wind stood up, and gave a shout;
> He whistled on his fingers, and
> Kicked the withered leaves about,
> And thumped the branches with his hand;
> And said he'd kill, and kill, and kill;
> And so he will! And so he will!

Peer-Response Form

Directions

1. Ask your partners to listen carefully as you read your rough draft aloud.

2. Ask your partners to help you improve your writing by telling you the answers to the questions below.

3. Jot down notes about what your partners say.

   a. What did you like best about my rough draft?

   b. What did you have the hardest time understanding about my rough draft?

   c. What can you suggest that I do to improve my rough draft?

4. Exchange rough drafts with a partner. In pencil, place a check mark near any mechanical, spelling, or grammatical constructions about which you are uncertain. Return the papers and check your own. Ask your partner for clarification if you do not understand or agree with the comments on your paper. Jot down notes you will want to remember when writing your revision.

Proofreading Guidesheet

1. Have you identified the assigned purpose of the writing assignment and have you accomplished that purpose?

2. Have you written on the assigned topic?

3. Have you identified the assigned form your writing should take and written accordingly?

4. Have you addressed the assigned audience in your writing?

5. Have you used sentences of different lengths and types to make your writing effective?

6. Have you chosen language carefully so the reader understands what you mean?

7. Have you done the following to make your writing clear for someone else to read:

   • used appropriate capitalization?

   • kept pronouns clear?

   • kept verb tense consistent?

   • made sure all words are spelled correctly?

   • used correct punctuation?

   • used complete sentences?

   • made all subjects and verbs agree?

   • organized your ideas into logical paragraphs?

Math: Probability of a Hurricane Hit

Purpose
To determine the probability of a hurricane hitting your selected city based on the past hurricane history of the city.

Materials
- Data table of hurricane hits
- Graph paper

Procedure
There were 745 Atlantic Ocean storms that reached tropical storm intensity or greater between 1900 and 1991. Of these, 301 crossed or passed along the coast of the United States, and 158 of them became hurricanes. Probability is calculated by dividing the favorable outcomes (the actual hurricane hits) by the total possible outcomes.

Use the data below to find the probability that the hurricane being studied by your team will hit each of the given cities in its path
1. using the total number of storms as the total outcome
2. using the storms that affected the United States as the total outcome
3. using the hurricanes that affected the United States as the total outcomes

Then construct a line plot or graph showing the frequency of hits in each month.

Data
Dates of hurricane hits for the following cities:

Mobile, Ala.
10/27/06; 8/11/11; 9/13/12; 9/20/26; 8/31/32; 10/30/50; 9/12/79

New Haven, Conn.
10/14/00; 9/21/38; 10/31/54; 9/12/60; 8/9/76; 9/27/85

Cedar Key, Fla.
10/25/21; 9/17/28; 9/2/35; 6/24/45; 10/18/68

Panama City, Fla.
10/31/03; 9/4/15; 9/15/24; 9/30/29; 8/26/39; 10/7/41; 9/26/53; 9/24/56; 6/19/72; 11/31/85

Pensacola, Fla.
7/11/01; 9/12/01; 9/17/01; 9/13/03; 8/11/11; 9/28/17; 9/20/26; 7/31/36; 9/26/53; 9/24/56; 9/23/75; 10/31/85

Biloxi, Miss.
8/15/01; 10/27/06; 9/13/12; 9/21/26; 8/361/32; 10/17/69; 7/12/79

Atlantic City, N.J.
9/16/03

Cape Hatteras, N.C.
7/11/01; 7/31/08; 9/3/13; 8/25/24; 8/23/33; 9/16/33; 9/18/36; 9/14/44; 8/13/53; 10/30/54; 8/12/55; 9/19/55; 9/27/58; 9/26/85; 6/17/86; 8/19/91

Corpus Christi, Tex.
6/26/02; 9/14/10; 10/16/12; 6/27/13; 8/16/15; 7/5/16; 8/18/16; 10/18/16; 9/14/19; 6/22/21; 6/27/36; 8/29/42; 9/11/61; 8/3/70; 9/10/71

Galveston, Tex.
9/8/00; 7/21/09; 8/16/15; 8/13/32; 9/23/41; 8/21/42; 7/27/43; 8/24/47; 10/4/49; 7/24/59; 9/17/63; 8/17/83; 6/26/86; 10/15/89; 8/1/89

Port Arthur, Tex.
8/7/40; 9/5/50; 6/27/57; 6/26/86; 8/1/89

Questions
1. Why did the probabilities for each city change as you did the different steps of the procedure?
2. Did the line plots for the cities in your hurricane's path show a specific month that hurricanes are more prevalent for your city?
3. Using the information in this activity, make a prediction as to which city will be hit by the hurricane. Support your prediction.
4. What other information do you need to increase the accuracy of your prediction? Why?

Social Studies: Be on the Lookout for Hurricanes!

Purpose

To construct a bar graph showing when during the year hurricanes are most likely to occur. To look at other extreme/severe forms of weather that occur in the United States (or the world) and determine when during the year they occur, the conditions necessary for their development, and the impact that these forms of extreme/severe weather have on people and the communities in which they live.

Materials

- Graph paper
- Hurricane data
- Research materials

Procedure

1. Review the hurricane data and record the frequency of hurricane occurrence by month.

2. Create a bar graph from the recorded data.

3. Develop a list of other extreme/severe forms of weather or the results of extreme/severe forms of weather that occur in the United States (or somewhere in the world).

4. The teacher, having developed a master list from the individual lists, will assign you to a group to research one of the other forms of extreme/severe forms of weather. The group task is to research this form of extreme/severe weather, show on a map where and when this weather is most likely to occur, and create a live, on-the-scene report from a part of the country (or world) that could experience such weather.

5. Determine which individual in your group will be the on-the-scene reporter. Determine the characteristics of the extreme/severe form of weather you plan to use. Use your creativity and imagination to determine the best way to display or suggest these characteristics.

6. The actual on-the-scene report must include the following:
   a. accurate description of weather characteristics
   b. suggestions for citizens to follow to prevent injury or property damage
   c. impact of the weather on the local community
   d. weather forecast

7. The on-the-scene report will be presented to the class.

Hurricanes, 1953–1986

1953
Barbara—August
Carol— August
Dolly—September
Edna—September
  Florence—September
  Gail—October

1954
Alice—June
Carol —August
Edna—August
Dolly—August
Florence—September
Hazel—October
Alice—December

1955
Connie—August
Diane—August
Edith—August
Flora—September
Gladys—September
Hilda—September
Ione—September
Janet—September
Katie—October

1956
Anna—July
Betsy—August
Flossy—September
Greta—October

1957
Audrey—June
Carrie—September
Frieda—September

1958
Cleo—August
Daisey—August
Ella—August
Fifi—September
Helene—September
Ilsa—September
Janice—October

1959
Cindy—July
Debra—July
Flora—September
Gracie—September
Hannah—September
Judith—October

1960
Abby—July
Cleo—August
Donna—August
Ethel—September

1961
Anna—July
Betsy—September
Carla—September
Debbie—September
Esther—September
Frances—September
Hattie—October
Jennie—November

1962
Alma—August
Daisey—September
Ella—October

1963
Arlene—July
Buelah—August
Cindy—September
Debra—September
Edith—September
Flora—September
Ginny—October

1964
Cleo—August
Dora—August
Ethel—September
Gladys—September
Hilda—September
Isbell—October

1965
Anna—August
Betsy—August
Carol—September
Elena—October

1966
Alma—June
Becky—July
Celia—July
Dorothy—July
Faith—August
Inez—September
Lois—November

1967
Arlene—August
Beulah—September
Chloe—September
Doria—September
Heidi—October

1968
Abby—June
Brenda—June
Dolly —August
Gladys—October

1969
Blanche—August
Camille—August
Debbie—August
Francelia—August
Gerda—September
Holly—September
Inga—September
Kara—October
Laurie—October

1970
Alma—May
Celia—July
Ella—September

1971
Beth—August
Edith—September
Fern—September
Ginger—September
Irene—September

1972
Agnes—June
Betty—August
Dawn—September

1973
Alice—July
Brenda—August
Ellen—September
Fran—October

1974
Becky—August
Carmen—August
Fifi—September
Gertrude—September

1975
Blanche—July
Caroline—August
Doris—August
Eloise—September
Faye—September
Gladys—September

1976
Belle—August
Candice—August
Emmy—August
Frances—August
Gloria—September
Holly—October

1977
Anita—August
Babe—September
Clara—September
Dorothy—September
Evelyn—October

1978
Cora—August
Ella—August
Flossie—September
Greta—September
Kendra—September

1979
Bob—July
David—August
Fredric—August
Gloria—September
Henri—September

1980
Allen—July
Bonnie—August
Charley—August
Earl—September
Frances—September
George—September
Ivan—September
Jeanne—November
Karl—November

1981
Dennis—August
Emily—August
Floyd—September
Gert—September
Harvey—September
Irene—September
Katrina—November

1982
Alberto—June
Debby—September

1983
Alicia—August
Barry—August
Chantal—September

1984
Dianna—September
Hortense—September
Josephine—October
Klaus—November
Lili—December

1985
Bob—July
Claudette—August
Danny—August
Elena—August
Gloria—September
Juan—October

1986
Bonnie—June
Charley—August
Earl—September
Frances—November

Beaufort Scale of Wind Forces

Beaufort Number	MPH	Explanatory Title	Visual Indicators
0	0	Calm	Calm, smoke rises vertically
1	1–3	Light air	Direction of wind shown by smoke drift, but not by wind vane
2	4–7	Slight breeze	Wind felt on face; leaves rustle, ordinary wind vanes moved by wind
3	8–12	Gentle breeze	Leaves and small twigs in constant motion; wind extends light flag
4	13–18	Moderate breeze	Raises dust and loose paper; small branches are moved
5	19–24	Fresh breeze	Small trees in leaf begin to sway; wavelets form on inland waters
6	25–31	Strong breeze	Large branches in motion; whistling heard in telegraph wires; umbrellas used with difficulty
7	32–38	High wind; moderate	Whole trees in motion; inconvenience gale felt when walking against the wind
8	39–46	Gale; fresh gale	Breaks twigs off trees; generally makes walking difficult
9	47–54	Strong gale	Slight structural damage occurs (chimney pots, shingles, and slate blown from rooftops)
10	55–63	Whole Gale	Seldom experienced on land; trees broken; structural damage occurs
11	64–72	Storm	Very rarely experienced on land; widespread damage
12	73 or higher	Hurricane force	Widespread destruction

BIBLIOGRAPHY

Books for Students:

Arco Editors. *Earth, Sea and Sky.* New York: Arco Publishing Company, 1984.

Branley, Franklyn M. *Hurricane Watch.* A Let's Read-And-Find-Out Science Book—for young readers. New York: Thomas Y. Crowell, 1985.

Cosgrove, Brian. *Weather.* New York: Alfred A. Knopf, 1991.

Goodman, Billy. *Natural Wonders and Disasters.* A Planet Earth book. Boston: Little, Brown and Company, 1991.

Helm, Thomas. *Hurricanes: Weather at its Worst.* New York: Dodd, Mead and Company, 1967.

Lambert, David, and Ralph Hardy. *Weather and its Work.* New York: Facts on File Publications, 1987.

Lane, Frank W. *The Violent Earth.* Topsfield, Mass.: Salem House, 1986.

Lockhart, Gary. *The Weather Companion: An Album of Meteorological History, Science Legend and Folklore.* New York: John Wiley and Sons, 1988.

Purvis, George, and Anne Purvis. *Weather and Climate.* New York: Bookwright Press, 1984

Schaefer, Vincent J., and John A. Day. *A Field Guide to the Atmosphere.* The Peterson Field Guide Series. Boston: Houghton Mifflin Company, 1981.

Simon, Seymour. *Storms.* Morrow Junior Books. New York: William Morrow and Company, 1989.

Simpson, Robert, and Herbert Riehl. *The Hurricane and Its Impact.* Baton Rouge, La.: Louisiana State University Press, 1981.

Williams, Jack. *USA TODAY's The Weather Book: An Easy-to-Understand Guide to the USA's Weather.* New York: Vintage/Random House, 1992.

Information about weather and climate:

American Meteorological Society, 1701 K Street N.W., Suite 300, Washington, D.C. 20006.

National Climatic Data Center, Federal Building, Asheville, N.C. 28801.

National Weather Service Public Affairs Office, 1325 East-West Highway, Silver Spring, Md. 20910.

Weatherwise, a bimonthly magazine, is for non-scientists who are interested in weather. It is published by Heldref Publications, 1319 18th Street N.W., Washington, D.C. 20036.

Acknowledgments

Author
Russell G. Wright, with contributions from Leonard David, Barbara Sprungman, and the following teachers:

Richard Chirumbole, West Middle School, Westminster, Maryland
Vivian H. Clyburn, Herbert Hoover Middle School*, Potomac, Maryland
Nell Jeter, Earle B. Wood Middle School*, Rockville, Maryland
Cynthia Johnson-Cash, Ridgeview Middle School*, Gaithersburg, Maryland
Jeanne S. Klugel, Col. E. Brooke Lee Middle School*, Silver Spring, Maryland
William R. Krayer, Gaithersburg High School*, Gaithersburg, Maryland
Marilyn Matthews, Gaithersburg Intermediate School*, Gaithersburg, Maryland
Carl Merry, Quince Orchard High School*, North Potomac, Maryland
Eugene M. Molesky, Ridgeview Middle School*, Gaithersburg, Maryland
John Senuta, Ridgeview Intermediate School*, Gaithersburg, Maryland
Sheila Shillinger, Montgomery Village Intermediate School*, Montgomery Village, Maryland
J. Martin Smiley, Gaithersburg Intermediate School*, Gaithersburg, Maryland
Clare E. Von Secker, Westland Middle School*, Bethesda, Maryland
Frank S. Weisel, Poolesville Junior/Senior High School*, Poolesville, Maryland

Event/Site Support
John Wickham, Coconut Creek, Florida; Althea King (Principal), Barbara Stinson, and students of Hammocks Middle School, Kendall, Florida; Harry La Cava (Principal), Mary Kay Lies, and students of Margate Middle School, Margate, Florida

Scientific Reviewers
Ed Rappaport, National Hurricane Center; Richard D. Marshall, National Institute of Standards and Technology

Student Consultants
Redland Middle School*, Rockville, Maryland: Julia Ahn, Amanda Armah, Jerard Barnett, Mark Batipps, Giancarlo Begazo, Twana Brooks, Dean Chilton, Jonathan Codell, Daniel Elbaz, Tim Lewis, Erin McMullen, Kym Thompson Ridgeview Intermediate School*, Gaithersburg, Maryland: Sean Shillinger, Jeffrey Hsii

Field-Test Teachers
Judith Basile and Karen Shugrue, Agawam Junior High School, Feeding Hills, Massachusetts
David Needham and Gloria Yost, Albert Einstein Middle School, Sacramento, California
Merah Burke, Edmonston-Westside High School, Baltimore, Maryland
Joanne Cannon and Adrianne Criminger, Lanier Middle School, Buford, Georgia
Cheryl Glotfelty and Von Mosser, Northern Middle School, Accident, Maryland
Rodney Clem and Elizabeth McDermott, Southern High School, Baltimore, Maryland
Mark Carlson and Amy Resler, Westlane Middle School, Indianapolis, Indiana

EBS Advisory Committee
Dr. Eddie Anderson, National Aeronautic and Space Administration
Ms. Mary Ann Brearton, American Association for the Advancement of Science
Dr. Lynn Dierking, National Museum of American History
Mr. Bob Dubill, *USA Today*
Mr. Herbert Freiberger, United States Geological Survey
Ms. Joyce Gross, National Oceanic and Atmospheric Administration
Dr. Harry Herzer, National Aeronautic and Space Administration
Mr. Frank Ireton, American Geophysical Union
Mr. Bill Krayer, Gaithersburg High School*
Dr. Rocky Lopes, American Red Cross
Dr. Jerry Lynch, John T. Baker Middle School*
Ms. Virginia Major, United States Geological Survey
Ms. Marylyn P. MacCabe, Federal Emergency Management Agency
Mr. John Ortman, United States Department of Energy
Dr. Noel Raufasté Jr., National Institute of Standards and Technology
Dr. Bill Sacco, Trianalytics Corporation
Mr. Ron Slotkin, United States Environmental Protection Agency

* Montgomery County Public Schools, Rockville, MD